GEORGE & **THE** MONSTER INSIDE

Book one of The Song of the Seraphim Chronicles

A.G. Hill

ISBN-13: 978-1500610708
ISBN-10 1500610704

First published 2009 as The Song of the Seraphim

www.andrewghill.com

www.facebook.com/the.books.ofA.G.Hill

Cover design: Cat Hill, chill-design.co.uk

GEORGE AND THE MONSTER INSIDE

Author's Guide on how to say:

Asebeia = as-ah-bee-ah!

Asebeian = as-ah-bee-an

Daionas = day-own-as

Zenobiel = zen-oh-be-al

Rûah = roo-hah!

Zillah = zill-ah

Eibsae = eeb-say

Seraphim = seh-rah-fim

Dedication

For Joyce, John, Ruth, Cathryn, Adam and Martin. Thanks for your encouragement, positive criticism and patience.

Chapter One

THE STRANGER IN THE STORM

The air was thick and humid, and the boy took a puff of his inhaler to relieve the tightness in his chest.

'Mum, I feel sick. Can I sit in the front?' he asked.

'Weakling!' snapped May. 'We've only just set off and you feel sick?'

'Shut your face!'

Their mother was trying to concentrate on driving; she sighed impatiently.

'She started it!'

'No I didn't! You're always going on about being ill. I bet you fake your asthma attacks to get sympathy.'

'Liar!'

'Rat face!'

'Fat face!'

'GEORGE!' snapped their mother. 'Apologise to your sister this instant!'

He mumbled a reluctant, 'Sorry!'

'I've enough to think about, without the two of you bickering. George can sit in the front after I've dropped May off at Rachel's. And, young lady, you ought to know better.'

'What have I done? He's always complaining – I bet he does make it up.'

'That's not true and you know it! Mum – tell her!'

The car stopped. Their mother turned and looked at them. The expression on her face was enough to still a hurricane. They remained quietly seething for the rest of the journey. When they reached their destination, their mother said, 'I want you two to promise me that you will not argue when your father is home. He'll be very tired from his journey and he'll need a lot of rest for the next few days. Do you understand?'

They answered together, 'We understand. We're sorry.'

'May,' continued their Mother, 'don't be out late, and make sure Rachel's dad gives you a lift home. Have you got your key?'

'Yes Mum,' sighed May, as she climbed out of the car. 'Can I go now?'

'I can't say I'm keen on this party, especially tonight. You be good and remember what I told you.'

May slammed the car door. 'Stop fussing Mum – Rachel's waiting!' She checked herself; slowly walked over to the driver's side. Bending to give her mother a kiss, she said,

'Sorry Mum. I'll be good. I promise.'

'Say goodbye to your brother.'

'Goodbye to your brother!'

George held back a giggle, 'That's original.' In response, May's tongue was briefly pointed in George's direction. His mood changed from resentful to playful.

'Fancy putting that back in your mouth.'

They waved to each other and George fastened the front seat belt. His mother gave him a travel sickness tablet before driving off. They headed for the country road. It would be an hour before they reached the motorway. George was still smarting from May's remarks.

'I don't make it up Mum.'

'Don't make what up?'

'My feeling sick.'

'I know that son; you don't have to convince me.'

He pouted his lip, 'Everyone says I'm a wimp.'

'Who's everyone?'

8

'Kids at school and May. Anyway, they're right – I am a wimp. I'm hopeless at sports, useless at maths, behind on everything and always getting ill. Nobody picks me for the football teams and I've no real friends and ...'

'Self-pity is a very ugly thing, George.' She glanced in his direction and ruffled his black hair. Then she replaced her hand on the wheel. 'You are not a wimp. You are not useless, nor are you a liar. However, don't try to gain sympathy through your illness.'

'What do you mean?'

'Don't go on about your problems all the time and don't worry about not having many friends. A person's worth is not in how popular they are, or how clever or rich, but in what choices they make.' George frowned,

'You've lost me, Mum.'

'For a start, you could have prevented that nasty argument with May if you had reacted to her differently. What I also mean is that the way someone faces difficulties reveals the kind of person they are. Take your nightmares for example; you've been having bad dreams for over a year now and you keep them to yourself – that shows courage, but it can be lonely being courageous.'

George's saucer-like eyes stared at his mother, 'How do you know I'm having nightmares?'

'I'm your mother... mothers know these things. Oh, just look at that sky!'

Angry dark clouds loomed overhead. Drops of rain bounced off the windscreen. George listened to the split-splat of water against the glass and to the wipers whining see-saw dance. They were on the main route to Gatwick airport. They were still some distance from the M23 but, despite the rain, the journey was quite smooth.

'Why is Dad arriving at Gatwick and not on a Hercules?'

'Hercules are for equipment and troops. Most personnel fly by commercial aircraft. You knew that, so don't change the subject.'

'What subject?'

9

'Okay, if you don't want to tell me about the dreams, that's up to you – though 'a problem shared is a problem halved' and I know that last night's was pretty nasty.'
George took a deep breath,
'Are you a witch?'
'No, I'm your mother and mothers know a lot about their children.' She smiled. 'Listen, I promise not to tell anyone – not even your father. You can't keep moaning and groaning at night without someone noticing. It might help if you tell me.'
He sighed deeply, 'Okay, but you promise not to tell anyone?'
'I've already promised.'
'I have the bad dreams every night. I feel as if I'm living two lives – one in this world and the other in a dream world.' His voice became softer and he muttered to himself, 'If you stay there long enough... you forget what music sounds like...' He fell silent but his thoughts continued, *no kinds of music at all... not a single tune to whistle in the dark, not even a note to brighten a sad face...*
The rain had become a deluge. Visibility was poor. The traffic slowed down and then stopped moving completely. An electronic signpost, high above the motorway, informed them that the road ahead was closed due to flooding. All vehicles were being instructed to leave the motorway at the next junction. They quickly studied a map.
'This is so B-O-R-ING!'
'I know son. I think the wheels have rusted. I know it's hard to believe, but we are moving.' She smiled at George and then said, 'You still haven't told me about your nightmares and what did you mean when you said, 'you forget what music sounds like?''
A flash of lightning pierced the sky. The thunder made George jump. In the distance a barn burst into flames.
'Wow!' exclaimed George, 'Look at that!' He pointed to thick, black clouds of smoke billowing into the air.

'See how big the flames are and the rain isn't even putting it out – that's amazing!'

'Okay, so you don't want to tell me now, perhaps later.'

Nothing was said for a while. His mother turned the radio on. She always had it tuned to Classic FM. George lost himself in the soothing sounds. She took the first left into a narrow country lane. The fact that the other cars had headed in another direction should have warned her that she had taken a wrong turn. The lane became narrower, twisting and turning around hedges and trees. There was only enough room for one car at a time, and very few passing places. She turned the windscreen wipers to double speed. They groaned at the amount of water they had to shift. The cascade made visibility zero. George couldn't make out the headlights of their car, let alone the lane. The water was so heavy the wipers gave up.

'This is hopeless,' said his mother. She stopped the car. 'I'll see if I can get the wipers to move.'

The wind blew the torrent in as she opened the door. The thunder boomed so loudly that it sounded like a cannon going off in the back seat. Streaks of lightning danced in the lane, skipping closer and closer to the car. George's heart missed a beat. He watched his mother trying to clear the windscreen. He jumped when he noticed a huge, dark shape beside him. It appeared to have a thousand tentacles, swaying back and forth.

'What's that?' he yelled, in near panic.

'It's only a tree,' she answered, as she got back into the car.

'Oh,' he said sheepishly. 'Don't go out there again, Mum, you're soaked to the skin.'

The music stopped. The lights went out. The engine died. She kept turning the key – it was useless. The car refused to start. George had gone pale. His mother reassured him,

'Don't worry, George, we'll be all right.' He wasn't convinced. There was a second when the rain eased. George sighed with relief. He shook when a sudden crash of thunder thumped on the roof. In a flash of light, he thought he saw the shadow of a giant in front of them. His mother rummaged in her handbag for her mobile.

'Bother! The battery's dead.'

A face appeared at the driver's window. George screamed. The man tapped on the glass.

'Don't be afraid,' he said, placing a wallet to the window. She relaxed when she saw the police badge, but George became tense. George's mother wound the window down slightly, just enough to speak to the stranger.

'Oh, officer, you gave us such a fright!'

'Sorry to make you jump – you look lost.'

'Yes, we are lost. We need the M23 for Gatwick and the car's broken down.'

'Okay, madam, open the bonnet, and I'll have a look.'

His yellow jacket shone in the flashes of lightning. They could make out that he was extremely tall. She remarked that if it were not for the jacket and police markings, she wouldn't have trusted him. George silently wondered whether they should trust him at all.

The bonnet was lifted. All George could see was the maroon paintwork. He stared at the tree again. It waved at him. There was something threatening in the way it swayed about and tapped the roof with its branches.

A brilliant flash of light broke the darkness. Oddly, it came from the direction of the engine. The old Escort jolted back to life. Music filled the air and the wipers resumed their dance. The stranger slammed the bonnet shut. He took something from his jacket pocket. It was a map.

'Follow this route and you'll be in Gatwick very soon. You will have to reverse the car. There's a passing place not far from here, in that direction.' He pointed to the way they had already come. 'When you get to the end of the lane, turn left, then take the first left. Move quickly now – farewell.'

'Thank you,' replied George's mother.

She was relieved when the car responded. It reversed slowly. George was glad to be away from the menacing tree. The explosion made them leap. A finger of lightning ripped the tree apart. Splinters scattered in all directions, snapping against the car. The tree twisted, branches flaying at the air. It crashed to the ground onto the very spot the car had just occupied. The lane was completely blocked. Without hesitating, both George and his mother got out of the car. They had the same thought – was the policeman safe?

'I can't see him!' George cried, through the thunder.

'Neither can I. In fact, there's no sign of him at all. It's as if he's vanished. Get back in the car, George.' He obeyed and she added, 'You know, that man saved our lives just then. If he hadn't fixed the car when he did, we'd be under that tree.'

'Yes I know… it's very strange.'

George didn't speak for the rest of the journey. The storm wore itself out. The thunder faded into the distance and the rain curled up in the clouds. He was afraid to speak because a different storm had awoken in George's mind. Fear and confusion whirled together. He had heard on the TV about people suffering from mental illness, seeing things that weren't there. Was there something wrong with him? Was he still dreaming? Was he having a problem separating real life from his daydreams and nightmares? He didn't dare tell his mother what he was thinking. She would never believe him if he told her that the policeman, who had just come to their aid, was a man he had seen in his nightmare.

Chapter Two

A DISTANT DAD

Dear Glen,

I'm sorry to hear about your parents splitting up. Will you still be living in Germany on the air base? When's your dad coming home? My Dad came home last week. I didn't recognise him at first because he was so thin. He looks skinny and I don't think he's very well. Mum says he's just tired, but I think he's been wounded. Mum and Dad won't tell me anything. I'm glad this war in the Middle East is finally over. Dad says that there's always some sort of trouble there, but he won't be sent back again.

May was in trouble because she came back home an hour after we did, and we got home at midnight! Mum went ballistic! I've never seen her so cross. It's my birthday in two weeks time and my brother John is coming home on leave. He's promised to take me to see his submarine in Scotland. I'm really looking forward to that because we're going to be staying in a hotel overnight.

Mind you, I'm not sure that I want to be eleven, because it means going up to senior school and I'm definitely not looking forward to that! Snooty Helen Risdale is going to go to the same senior school as me! I wish she'd gone to boarding school. She still picks on me. I'll never forgive her for spoiling my birthday last year. I hate Helen! She's always boasting about her dad being an officer and a pilot and making fun of me because my Dad's a chef, but he had to go to war too and I bet he was wounded.

Anyway, I've got to finish now.
Your best friend,
George.

George's brother couldn't keep his promise, because the Navy didn't give him leave until after George's birthday. However, he did give George some money. George used it to buy another engine for his train set.

The first weeks after his father's return were contented and relaxed. On the night before John went back to his vessel, he took the family out for a meal. They met Jacqueline, George and May's older sister, at the restaurant. George managed not to argue with May for most of the evening. He kept glancing at his parents. He had noticed his mother becoming more and more tense. The reason became clear when George saw how much his father was drinking. At the door of the restaurant, his parents spoke sharply to each other. George was surprised when John and his father went to the Sergeants' Mess. George whispered to May, 'Why's Dad going to his work at this time of night?'

'I don't know – perhaps there's people working nights.'

Jacqueline, overhearing them, explained, 'The Mess room isn't just where dinners are served. In the evenings it's a social club – they have gone for a drink. Mum is upset because he has had too much to drink already.'

'But,' added May, 'Dad's never gone there for a drink before.'

Jacqueline put her finger to her lips. 'It would be better if you two went straight to bed when you get home. Mum needs some time alone.' When they arrived home, they did as Jacqueline suggested and dashed upstairs to their rooms.

16

George placed his head on his pillow and fell into a deep sleep. Raised voices in the middle of the night woke him up. He slid out of bed and crept to the door. May was leaning over the banister, her hair untidy and her pyjamas crumpled. George joined her. She was startled when he asked her what she was doing.

'Oh! You gave me a fright!' she hissed.

She motioned with her finger for him to be quiet. He peered over the banisters and saw that his father was on the floor. John and his mother were trying to help him up.

'Is he ill?' George whispered to May.

She screwed up her pretty face in disgust. 'He's drunk!' She moved away. 'I'm going back to bed and you'd better too, if you don't want to get caught.'

George was left alone on the landing. He couldn't believe what he was seeing – his father swayed and staggered, unable to stand without help. Sometimes he would laugh, then cry and mutter something George couldn't hear.

It was clear that John and his mother were trying unsuccessfully to get his father up the stairs. In the end they placed him in a chair. George heard his mother saying to John, 'You put the sofa bed out, while I go and get the bedding.'

He ran back into his room and climbed under the quilt. He was confident that his mother hadn't seen him. 'George,' she said quietly, through the closed door. 'Go back to sleep. Everything will be all right.'

George sat up, shaking his head in amazement. The door opened and her gentle face greeted him, 'Don't be too hard on your father, he needs our love and understanding just now.'

George didn't understand what was going on, even so he obeyed his mother and closed his eyes. He drifted off into a disturbed and restless sleep.

The weeks passed; school ended, much to George's delight. Life seemed to return to normality. Most of the school holidays were spent in his room, playing.

The train layout, his father had made for him, was so good that some other boys on the RAF base came to see it. News got around that George Tweedie had the best model railway in Fordale. It even lured boys away from their computer games and televisions. In a way that he had never expected, his hobby helped George make some new friends.

The summer holidays were flying by because he was having so much fun. One afternoon, George bounded up the stairs, followed by two friends, eager to play on the railway. One of them had not seen the set before and was greatly excited. George stood outside his bedroom, ready to thrust open the door and show off his amazing train set.

'Is it really that good?' asked the boy.

'It's brilliant,' answered George and the other boy together.

George's smile filled his face, but then he opened the door and his smile fell off. The track that had surrounded the room was in pieces. There was no sign of the wooden base. The hills, tunnels and buildings were bits of broken clay lying in a heap on the floor. The tracks and models were placed on George's bed.

'Haven't you bothered to put it together?' demanded the new boy.

George couldn't answer. The boy who had seen the set before said something kind, and led his companion out of the house. George couldn't believe his eyes; tears began to sting them. His father's voice came from behind him, jolting him back to life.

'Ah, there you are, George. Help me get this table into your room, will you. You can put your set on this.' George took hold of one end of a small table and helped his father place it beside a wall. He realised that he would only be able to put a tiny fraction of the set on the table top.

He listened, as though in a trance, to his father telling him, 'I need the wood, you see… to make a china cabinet. You still have the floor, and I'm sure your imagination could make something of the bits of clay.'

George slumped onto his bed. Pain gripped his chest. The anger welled up inside him and bubbled through his eyes and down his hot cheeks. For the first time in his life, George didn't like his father. His mother did her best to comfort him. She held him tight, caressing his hair and getting him to breathe slowly.

That evening, she helped him re-arrange the train set. George had to put most of it away in boxes and used only a part of the layout. He asked his mother to remove the table, because he couldn't bear to see it. The china cabinet his father made was splendid, but George gave it a kick every time he went past it. He wrote to Glen, telling him how he hated his father for what he had done and how he was fed up seeing his father getting blind drunk nearly every night. Glen replied to George, but he had more bad news.

Dear George,

Thanks for your letters. Sorry to hear about the train set and the way your dad is behaving. Parents can be such a pain, can't they? My parents told me that they are getting a divorce. Now they are arguing who is going to look after me. I'm trying to be so good that both of them will want me and they'll stay together. I don't like the man Mum now wants to marry, and I don't want to live with him. I'm going to try to get my parents together again. I hope I succeed. Sorry that this letter won't cheer you up.

Your pal, Glen.

Glen was correct – the letter only added to George's gloom. George couldn't help wondering what he had done to his father to make him change. Each day the tension in the home mounted. His parents had started to have major quarrels, and whenever they argued, George took to his room. He huddled in a corner, listening to his father ranting about the lack of money. He had seen his father thrust a bill under the nose of his mother so often that he knew that the safest place to be was in his bedroom.

He sat on the floor, in the corner by the door. He clutched the model of the Flying Scotsman, trying desperately to ignore the shouting.

Downstairs his mother glanced upwards, in the direction of George's room; her deep blue eyes were brimming with tears for both her husband and her son. She never said a word when her husband blamed her for the lack of finance.

'It's that car of yours,' he yelled. 'It's costing us a fortune. Petrol, tax, garage bills – you don't need it now.'

A few days later the car was sold and George's father used the money they got for it to start a new hobby. He came home late from work one evening, having bought a rusty antique sword. His father held the curved sword in the air and said,

'It's an American cavalry sabre like the ones you see in old cowboy films.' He worked on the sword, sanding it down to remove the rust, sharpening the edge and polishing it until he could see his face in it. He created a special mount to hang it on the wall. The light coming through the window opposite made the sword sparkle. 'Look at that!' he beamed. 'What do you think of it George?'

'It's cool.'

His mother made only one comment.

'Don't go near it, George, in case it falls off the wall.'

'Oh stop fussing, Grace!' snapped his father. 'It is very secure. I made sure of that. It does look lonely, though.' He went over to the music centre, unplugged it, and then put it in a box. After placing his large collection of CDs in another box, he went out. He returned with two more swords.

George had never thought his father would lose his interest in music. He and May played a game of guessing what their father would sell next in order to enlarge his growing collection. There were blades from many different ages, ranging from Roman times to the present day. The swords came from different parts of the world.

George couldn't help but marvel at the exotic weapons that now hung on the living room wall. He observed his mother hiding her earnings from her work, so that she could use it for the housekeeping. He made sure they were alone when he asked her why his father was behaving in this strange manner.

She patted the arm of the chair she was sitting in and put down her book. George sat beside her and she placed her arms around him. As usual, she sensed his deepest worries.

'It is nothing that you have done, George. Your father still loves you and the rest of the family, though at the moment he has a troubled soul. He needs our love and patience in these difficult days.'

'He's been acting weird ever since he came back from that war.'

'You are right, but I can't tell you why at the moment, because you are not ready. When you are ready, you will be the one to help your father.'

George was puzzled. 'Me? How can I help him?'

'By trying to love him and understand him.'

He prised himself away from her. He paced up and down the room, holding a silent argument with himself. Finally, he said what he was feeling. 'I hate him!'

'Oh, son, don't say that.'

'But I do – I hate it when he shouts at you and blames you for things he's done. I wish…'

He bit his lip and ran up the stairs. George tried to understand what his mother had told him. He watched his father closely, looking deep into the dark eyes gazing into the distance. Though his father's body was in the house, his mind and heart appeared to be in an entirely different place. Every time his father went out in the evening, George dreaded his return, knowing that he would come back drunk. May tried to cope with her father's behaviour by staying out with friends or playing video games. Sometimes she watched TV with the volume on high. That only made matters worse.

The house they lived in didn't have a back door. It had patio doors, leading directly into the garden. One Saturday, the doors were open to cool the room. George was in the garden kicking a ball around. The ball bounced into the living room on more than one occasion, much to May's annoyance.

'I'll keep it next time it comes in.'

George ignored her. He needed the distraction of messing about with a ball. It helped to get his mind off the fact that his mother was away. She was looking after Jacqueline, who was unwell. He had become nervous of his father who was looking after them for the weekend. He kicked the ball – it flew into the room and bounced off the television.

'That's it – I'm keeping it this time!'

'Give it back – it's mine!'

'Oh no,' she goaded. 'It's mine now.' She ran into the garden and George chased her. He tried to prise the ball away from her grasp.

They struggled, then fell on the ground in a tussle. The shadow of their father made them freeze.

'What's going on?' he demanded.

'May's taken my ball and won't give it back!'

'It's my ball now – he gave it to me!'

'That's a lie!'

Their father silenced them with a growl. He held out his huge hand and May placed the ball into it. They followed him into the living room. He took a curved dagger off the wall. Without a word, he placed the ball on the floor and cut the ball in half. Carefully, he replaced the dagger.

'Hold out your hands,' he said, and gave them a half each. 'Now it belongs to both of you.'

He turned away and went back into the kitchen. Their jaws dropped and they stared at the divided ball. Simultaneously, they burst out laughing. The giggling fit lasted a long time. They huddled together on the sofa and watched TV. Later they decided to visit their father in the kitchen. He laughed at the sight of them because they were both wearing a half of the ball on their heads.

'Thanks for the hats, Dad!'

'Very fetching – set the table for me, lunch is nearly ready.'

Before doing as he asked, they apologised for arguing. They felt as if the old, happy times had returned. However, after lunch, the children were asked to do the dishes. They squabbled about whose turn it was to wash up.

Their father settled the argument by hurling all the dishes in the dustbin. He lost his temper and shouted at them. They backed away in terror as he moved towards them but he had no intention of hitting them; he didn't even see them as he headed for the front door.

The door slammed and they watched their father from the landing window. He was marching down the road.

'I bet he's going for a beer!' spat May. 'I hate him!'

Very deliberately, George said,

'So...do...I.' He paused as he stared at his father disappearing into the distance. 'That's not our Dad. It's as if someone sent back a hideous clone of him from the Middle East.'

Chapter Three

UNWANTED INFORMATION

The holidays were over. George was in a new school facing an old enemy. Helen Risdale wore a crooked grin on her pretty face.

'Hello George – guess what? We are in the same class; now isn't that good? Ah, have I just spoiled your day? Did you have a good holiday in your garden? Playing the silent game are you? Well, I had a wonderful holiday in the Bahamas and I bought you a present.'

She held out a pickle jar full of worms. George's face betrayed his fear but he held his ground.

'Well, scream and run away! What are you looking at?'

A hand reached over Helen's shoulder and snatched the jar away. She spun round to see May unscrewing the lid.

'Get her bag, Rachel.' Before Helen could do anything, the worms were squirming over Helen's packed lunch. She screeched in horror and ran. May shouted after her, 'If you can't take it, don't dish it out! You're small fry in this school. And tell your friends no one picks on my little brother except me.'

George laughed until his sides ached. May scowled at him, 'Now scram – I don't want you hanging around me, okay?' George nodded and wandered to his classroom still laughing. Helen never bothered him again.

Mrs Tweedie got a job delivering meals to the elderly in the village. She would give George and May a lift home in the van she used; they waited for her at the home of a family friend called Mr Johnson. One afternoon they were enjoying his company and a large tin of chocolate biscuits. May was pouring the tea and Mr Johnson was piling George's plate with biscuits.

'I thought you couldn't eat chocolate,' mumbled George, who had a glass of milk in one hand and sticky fingers on the other.

'I can't eat chocolate.'

'Then how come,' George reached for another digestive, 'you've got chocolate biscuits in?'

'I knew you were coming.'

'He's very intelligent, isn't he May?'

She nodded. Her mouth was full. She handed a cup of tea to her mother and to her host. Mr Johnson winked at their mother.

'I think now would be a good time, my dear.'

The children frowned. They wondered what the time was good for. The look on their mother's face warned them that she was going to say something they didn't want to hear. She said it anyway.

'Two days ago, your father received orders to move to RAF Biggton in Kent.' She let the news sink in before saying, 'George, take your biscuit out of the milk. May, you look like a fish trying to catch flies. Don't you purse your lips at me, young lady!'

'Now, my dear,' interrupted the old man. 'There's no need for conflict. Tell her about my plan.'

Looks of curiosity replaced their frowns. Their mother relaxed, 'I'm sorry, May. None of us want to leave and it's going to be difficult for us all. I know it's going to be hard for both of you to change schools. I will help you, George, to adjust as best as I can. And you my dear...' she placed her hand on May's, 'have a wonderful opportunity before you. This dear old gentleman has connections with an excellent boarding school in Sussex.'

Their mother became excited as she told them, 'The school have funds available for children of armed forces personnel. I didn't know this, but Mr Johnson was a teacher at that school. He knows the headmaster very well. The head has been in touch with your school and what they had to say about you impressed him.'

She paused and beamed proudly at May, then said, 'He was told that your work is outstanding and that you should excel in your exams. You'll be fourteen soon, and attending a boarding school means that your education will not suffer when the RAF moves us again. You'll be able to stay on at the school until you are eighteen, if you want to.'

Mr Johnson gave May a booklet all about the school and added, 'You will have to sit a little entrance exam, but you'll have no bother passing that.'

May didn't say a word. Her face betrayed her mixed emotions; she didn't want to leave home, but as she looked through the booklet, she became more interested in the school.

'You don't have to decide now,' he said, 'though I think you would agree with us that this is a golden opportunity.'

In reply, she thanked the old man with a hug. Mr Johnson looked with concern at George, who was lost in thought, and said, 'What do you think, young man?'

'I think it's great – I'll be rid of my bossy sister!'

May poked her tongue out at George. 'And I'll be rid of you!'

'Don't start, you two!' snapped their mother. Then she looked at her son's worried face. 'I'm sorry, George, but we couldn't get a place for you; besides the school wouldn't be suitable because of your health.'

Mr Johnson leaned over to George and placed a hand on his shoulder. 'If you want to go to the school, you could take the exam and I'm sure your health wouldn't be a problem.'

'I'd fail the exam because I'm thick!'

The old man looked straight into George's eyes. 'Don't you ever think that about yourself! You are an intelligent boy.'

George screwed up his face in disbelief. 'Anyway, I don't want to go to boarding school – I don't want to go to *any* school ever again!' Everyone laughed out loud and the children helped themselves to more biscuits.

Preparations for the move got under way. George packed his toys. He took extra care with the train set, marking the box clearly. He wanted that to be the first box he unpacked. The activity of getting ready for the move had a positive effect on everybody. Problems were forgotten in the promise of a new start.

May had fallen in love with the boarding school when she had gone to see it. She passed the entrance exam with no difficulty and, when the school offered her a place, she decided to go.

Not long after May left, George overheard his mother talking on the telephone to Mr Johnson: 'That school is the best thing that's happened to May. I hope it will point her in the right direction and focus that intelligent mind of hers. Unfortunately, there is only one school near Biggton that I can send George to, and I'm not impressed with it.'

He didn't like the sound of that one little bit. He remembered something that his father had once told him.

'Avoid eavesdropping, son, because you might pick up information you don't want.'

On the day of the move, George stood in his room. It was empty, apart from the bed, a dressing table and a locker that all belonged to the RAF. For the fifth time that day, he checked the built-in wardrobe. There were no toys left on the shelves or lost in a corner. He slid the doors shut, then checked the locker and the drawers of the dressing table. He was reluctant to leave the room.

'Goodbye room. I'm going to miss you.' His voice echoed, so he said goodbye again. He couldn't resist one final look out of the window.

'Bye runway. Bye planes.'

He was going to miss the sight of the Hercules soaring into the air or coming home to rest. From his viewpoint, the aircraft looked like toys. He had often felt that he could reach out his hand, take hold of one, and run around the room with it.

Placing his elbows on the windowsill, he gazed wistfully at the descending clouds. He fancied that they took on the shape of a huge castle, floating high above the runway. 'I'm really going to miss this place.' George was startled by how loud the echo had become.

He shivered. The room was cold, despite it being a sunny day. The windowsill felt rough. Stony points dug into his elbows. He looked down and saw rocks instead of pine floorboards. His knees were wet from the muddy puddle he was kneeling in. He jumped up and banged his head on stone.

'Ow!' he yelped. 'What's going on? I'm... I'm – in a cave!'

Cold wind blew through the cave mouth. George looked out and saw ancient, dirty skyscrapers looming over a forbidding city. The cloud continued to form the shape of a castle. Shafts of sunlight were piercing the clouds, giving the impression that the castle was made out of gold. Something moved behind him. He spun around to face the shadows.

'Who's there?' he said in a thin and trembling voice.

His skin was tight and prickly. His breathing speeded up. He reached for the inhaler in his pocket but dropped it. As he bent down to pick it up, a massive claw pounced on it. A loud thud bounced around the cave. There was another thud. There were two claws in front of him now.

He heard heavy breathing, and then felt warm air against his face. His eyes smarted as the foul breath enveloped him. He forced his eyes to stay open. Piercing, bloodshot eyes bore into his from a massive hairless head that now hovered over George. The cruel face had strange features. The curved fangs were the size of carving knives. The neck was lithe and snake-like.

The body was mostly hidden in darkness – thick, heavy, oppressive darkness. A glimmer of light cut the dark and George thought he saw crab-like legs. It was impossible to see the creature properly.

George felt his insides toss and turn, the taste of sick came into his mouth. He tried to speak, but couldn't. His legs were blocks of ice. His mind was still active, and now he understood why no one ran away in scary films.

The hideous voice set George's teeth on edge. It was a deep, throaty whisper, with the hint of a hiss.

'You are in my domain.' A forked tongue flashed out at him. 'I have your father and your sisster. Soon you will be mine. Soon you will live in my city. Then you will feast on dessspair.'

A flicker of light from outside the cave danced in the corner of George's eye. He found his voice.

'Who are you?'

It spoke in slow motion. 'I... am... the... king... The Only King.' The claws glided towards George's head. 'The ruler of shadowss – that is who I am.'

George thought that the powerful talons were going to squeeze his head like an orange. He picked up a rock from the cave floor.

'Go away!' The rock bounced harmlessly off a pointed ear.

'You will join me. You will ssserve me. You will be mine – jusst like your father!'

George threw another stone. He fell on his hands and knees, crawling away from the claws. The creature twisted its neck. The jaws opened, dripping foul spittle. George closed his eyes, waiting to be swallowed.

A warm light kissed his face. He looked up and saw a vast golden city hovering in the sky. Beautiful, unearthly voices flooded the cave. The city was full of song. George could only hear the word 'Daionas.' It brought fear to the creature.

As the song grew in strength, the creature faded into the shadows. George sighed with relief.

Suddenly the creature's face was thrust in front of him.

'I am with you always, George Tweedie. With you always, watching and waiting... alwaysss.'

Another voice spoke, 'Do not believe him, George. He is lying to you. Listen to my voice, and leave the shadows George... George.' A massive, dark-skinned man stood at the bedroom door. 'You are George Tweedie, aren't you?' George swallowed. 'Yes.'

The man had a strong, kind, brave face. He wore an American air force uniform and spoke with a soft American accent. 'You looked miles away there, sonny. Sorry to make you jump.'

'No, it wasn't you who made me jump.'

'Pardon?'

'Oh, nothing. What do you want?'

The man took one stride and then stood before George. He bent down and waved a large brown envelope under George's nose. 'I've come to give your father this.'

'He's already left, but I'll give it to my Mum; she's loading my sister's car.'

'Would you? That would be swell.'

He patted George on the head, then left.

'Hang on a minute!' yelled George, running down the stairs, 'You're that policeman – the one who helped us when the car broke down!' He ran into his mother. 'Oops!' she laughed, 'what's the hurry and who were you shouting at?'

'That airman.'

'What airman? I never saw anybody. George, are you all right?'

'Er... yes,' he said dreamily, 'the... er... airman came to give you this.' He handed her the packet.

She gave her son a questioning look. 'I've had this for a week, son; it's only papers about the move.'

Chapter four

OLD PROBLEMS IN NEW PLACES

Ever since the teacher had entered the classroom, the atmosphere had been electric. The boys worked in silence. At first glance, the elderly man appeared harmless. His pleasant, kindly face was covered in a thick white beard and he resembled a small Father Christmas without the red suit. The teacher hadn't spoken for a full five minutes.

He startled everyone when he said, 'What is that smell?' His voice was calm and authoritative. He sniffed the air. 'Smoke – definitely smoke.' He didn't smile or sneer; his face remained kind. He picked up a wooden ruler and walked down the rows of desks. He suddenly sniffed a boy's head. 'I thought I could smell burning wood. The lot of you would make Pinocchio look like Einstein.'

'Who's that?' whispered George to the boy sitting next to him. 'I haven't seen him before.'

'He's been away. His name is Mr Stenching – Adolph Hitler in disguise.'

The teacher spun round, but was too late to see who had spoken. However, he did spot a new victim. He moved slowly to the back row and stood in front of George, who tried to ignore the teacher and continue with his work. The ruler was forced under his chin compelling him to raise his head. He looked into the cold green eyes.

'A new boy? What is your name, boy?'

'Tweedie, sir.'

'TWIT WEE… That's an unusual name.'

The other boys sniggered. George's stomach churned.

'My name is Tweedie, sir.'

'Spell it for me.'

'T-w-e-e-d-i-e.'

The teacher shook his head, sighed deeply and asked, 'How old are you, boy?'

'Eleven, sir.'

Once again the teacher shook his head, 'Eleven-years-old… and you still do not know how to spell your own name! It is spelt T-w-e-e-d-y.'

'No, sir, there's more than one way to spell the name and our family's name ends with an 'I-E.'

'Did you say 'No sir', to me?'

Mr Stenching's face was so close to George's that their noses almost touched. 'No-one contradicts me, Tweedledee. Or should that be Tweedledum?' George was relieved when the malevolent teacher straightened up, though he couldn't take his eyes off the ruler. The teacher's supple fingers playfully twisted the ruler round and round. 'Look at me when I am speaking to you, Tweedie.'

George looked into the snake-like eyes and a smile slid over Mr Stenching's face.

'You are a new boy… so… I will be merciful. When did you come to this school?'

'Three weeks ago, sir.'

'The middle of November is an odd time to start school, Tweedledum. Where have you been hiding all term?'

George's voice was hoarse. 'I haven't been hiding, sir. We've just moved to RAF Biggton.'

'So you are an Air Force brat? – answer me, boy!'

'Y…yes, sir.'

'Tweedie – that's Irish isn't it?'

'It's Scottish, sir.'

'Scottish?'

George nodded, but the teacher shook his head.

'No. I think that you will find that the name is Irish.'

I think I ought to know if my name is Scottish or not! thought George.

'What is ten percent of twenty two pounds?'

George's tummy flipped over. Could this nasty little man read minds? No. He'd seen his reports. He had read that maths was George's weakest subject. He knew exactly where to twist the knife. George realised that it was useless trying to guess. He sighed, 'I don't know, sir. I've been getting help for maths in my last school.'

The teacher puffed up his chest and he smiled broadly. He pointed to the chief bully in the class. 'You there! – Stipe, give him the answer.'

'Two pounds, twenty pence, sir.'

'You see, Tweedledum, even Stipe knew the answer.' Mr Stenching became quiet. He was motionless though all his muscles were tense. He stared directly into George's eyes.

George stared back without blinking. All the sniggering stopped. The entire class was like a football crowd, waiting in awed silence, for the final penalty shoot-out. The boys looked from Mr Stenching's face to the ruler that he was flicking, like a serpent's tongue. They all knew what would happen if George blinked. But he didn't blink. The class was transfixed by the sight of the crimson-faced boy out-staring the teacher.

Mr Stenching was poised like a cobra intimidating its prey. The class had never witnessed such a long duel of wits. There was a glimmer of respect for the new boy. Now Mr Stenching's face was red; his eyes started to water – and he blinked. He lashed out with the ruler. George felt the rush of air against his face as the ruler struck the desk. George didn't make a sound. He showed no emotion. Mr Stenching swallowed and walked to his desk, rapping it with the ruler to gain the class's attention.

'You are all wooden-tops. I am profoundly relieved that I do not have to teach you every day – just sitting in for Mr Phelps. Get on with whatever work he gave you to do ... and Tweedie...' He waited for George to look at him, smiled pleasantly, and said, 'Welcome to the school.'

Everyone looked down again. George's cheeks smouldered like a barbecue. He breathed in and out slowly, and the tightness within his chest eased. George was relieved that he didn't have to use his inhaler. The last time he had used it in class, Stipe had snatched it from him and then sprayed the medicine into his eyes. It didn't harm him, but it was unpleasant. George shot a glance in Mr Stenching's direction. The teacher was lost in thought.

George added Mr Stenching to the mental list of bullies he was keeping. George hated every second, every minute, every hour and every day of his time at Dunhill Senior School for boys. He expressed his hatred by re-naming the school, Dunghill. He was the outsider, the only boy in his class from RAF Biggton, which was ten miles away. He kept glancing at Stenching while he recalled the previous three weeks with a shudder. He had been threatened with a knife and a chisel; hit on the head with a heavy folder and spat upon by several members of his class, led by Stipe. The last was a particularly nasty memory...

As usual, at some point in the day, the classroom was left without supervision. The school had difficulty keeping staff and had to rely on supply teachers who didn't care. George had been sitting with his back to Stipe, who commented on George's new blazer.

'I like your blazer, Tweedie.'

George grunted, 'Thanks,' hoping that Stipe would occupy his twisted mind with something else, but Stipe said, 'I always thought that black was a boring colour. Wouldn't you agree, Rankling?'

Rankling was a spotty-faced boy who agreed with everything Stipe said. Stipe sneered, 'I think that green is a much better colour.'

The laughter poured out like pus bursting from a boil. George's arms were pinned to the desk. There was no escape from the deluge of spit and phlegm. Soon George was covered in the filth. They taunted as they spat, 'Don't you like gob, Tweedie? Thought kids like you ate snot.' When the classroom door opened, the mob broke up.

The Head Teacher stood in the doorway. He was a feeble, balding man in his late forties. He treated all the boys as if they were reasonable human beings.

'Now, now, sit down, all of you.'

When he saw the state of George's blazer, he shook his head. 'Tut-tut. This isn't the way to treat a new boy. Who did this?'

No one answered. George didn't dare say.

'Well, you'll all have to stay in for detention.' He looked sadly at George and sighed, 'Tweedie, go and get cleaned up and don't let them do that to you again…'

George stopped day-dreaming when he saw Mr Stenching staring at him. The teacher was about to say something when the bell rang to announce the end of morning lessons. After lunch, George stood in front of the wooden woodwork hut – the site of his first encounter with Stipe, who had threatened him with a sharp chisel. George stared at the hut and went through his now-daily ritual.

He mentally placed half the school, including teachers, into the woodwork room. He could see it all clearly. The room was locked. There was no escape. A Harrier Jump Jet would zoom overhead. The deafening roar of rockets made the cries of those inside impossible to hear. Then the whole building would be blown to bits – but only in his imagination.

George was glad when the school day was finally over. As he approached the school gates, his jaw dropped when he saw his father waiting for him.

'Dad? What are you doing here?'

'I came with Corporal Scrum to pick you up. You're not going home on the bus tonight.'

George saw the corporal's Ford Focus, and was impressed. However, he couldn't help the feeling of impending doom, so he asked,

'But why have you come to pick me up Dad?'

'Point out the bully who keeps picking on you. Which one is Stipe?' George was stunned. He didn't answer, so his father demanded, 'Point him out, boy!'

'Er…he's over there. He's the dark-haired boy built like a brick, stuffing his face with chocolate.'

George pointed to Stipe.

'Get in the car.'

As George obeyed the order, a giant of a man emerged from the car. He confronted Stipe and lifted him off the ground with one arm. The chocolate bar plopped to the ground. Stipe's face was ghost-like. The whole incident only took seconds, but to George, watching from the car, it seemed as if a lifetime was passing. He couldn't help feeling a certain pleasure in seeing Stipe squirm, but he knew that this was going to end in more misery for him. Within minutes of arriving, his father and Corporal Scrum were back in the car. On the homeward journey they were congratulating themselves for 'sorting out the bully.'

'He'll not bother you again, son.'

George's mother was furious when her husband told her what he and Corporal Scrum had done.

'You could be arrested – what on earth were you thinking?'

'There's no danger of being arrested.'

'You don't know that. The boy's parents could call the police.'

'Don't worry, love. The boy will be too scared to tell anyone. Besides, we made sure that we weren't seen.'

'You don't know that.'

George's father threw his beer glass across the room. 'What is this? I go to the aid of your precious son and this is all the thanks I get!' He stormed out of the house. The slam of the door was as loud as thunder.

George's mother sighed deeply. 'We'll not see him for the rest of the evening. Better be in bed when he comes home.'

'But Mum...' George hesitated, 'It was great seeing Stipe dangle from that huge arm. He deserved it. He got a taste of his own medicine.' He looked into her mournful eyes and noticed how long and thin her face was becoming. She sighed again.

'Violence breeds violence. Revenge feeds hatred.'

'But Mum, what about wars? I heard someone on the TV say that wars can be right sometimes, because you have to fight evil. Isn't that true?'

'George, you know very well that I'm not talking about that. I'm talking about an eleven-year-old boy being threatened by a grown man.'

'He deserved it.'

'Did he? Whatever he's done to you does not give you the right to bully him. If you resort to bullying, then you are no different to Stipe.'

George went into the kitchen for a glass of milk. He had been wrestling with himself whether to tell his mother about Mr Stenching threatening him with a ruler. In the end he decided he would tell her as she came into the kitchen to prepare dinner. He took a deep breath.

'Mum... I met Mr Stenching today.'

'Yes, I know. He phoned me to say that he has been away on a conference, so he hasn't had the chance to see you until today. I met him when I enquired about a place for you in the school. He's such a nice man, isn't he?'

George's brain had become scrambled eggs – he couldn't think of a thing to say, except to ask nervously,

'Why did he phone you?'

'Well, it was very thoughtful, really. He wanted to tell me how impressed he was by you and to assure you not to worry about your maths, because he will be giving you special attention. I thought that was very kind of him.' She smiled broadly. 'Don't be so glum. I think it's wonderful that he wants to take care of you.'

Fear slithered down his spine at the words 'special attention' and 'take care of you.' *Mum will never believe me now*, he thought. *Stenching's made it impossible for me to say anything bad about him. Grown-ups are better bullies than kids – they're as crafty as snakes.*

George was glad that the next day was Saturday and there was no school for two whole days. He woke with a start. The curtains in his room were flapping about. The wind whistled through the gaps in the window. He missed his old room with its double glazing and warm floorboards. The floor in his new room was covered in a worn grubby carpet. There was only enough room for a bunk bed and locker. The wardrobe was small and there was hardly any space for his toys. George didn't like this place he was forced to call home.

He didn't like RAF Biggton either. It was a base that was in the process of being closed down. There was no active runway and the houses were very old. It was a mystery to him why his father had been stationed there.

George had been distressed to discover, on the very first day after the move, that his beloved train set and model planes had not completed the journey. The toys, along with Mrs Tweedie's large collection of books, had mysteriously disappeared. His father had travelled with the RAF truck carrying their belongings. He explained that the truck had broken down and they had to transfer everything into another truck. In the confusion some boxes were mislaid. As George stared at the wardrobe, a nagging thought re-surfaced that his father was somehow to blame for the loss of his things, especially as his father's sword collection had survived the move.

He yawned and stretched, then went to the bathroom. The landing was small and the bedroom doors were close to each other. On his return, George clearly heard sobbing. He stood at his parents' room. The door was ajar and George's curiosity got the better of him. *What's going on?*

Why is Dad crying like a baby? And Mum's holding him and stroking his head like she does with me when I'm upset. I wonder what she's saying. Why's he like this? What's going on? Better stay out of their way today and watch TV. He never made a sound as he crept back to his own room and got dressed. He tip-toed down the stairs and got his own breakfast. At 9.30, the post came – there was a letter from Glen.

Dear George,

I couldn't get my parents together and they've got divorced. They are fighting for custody of me now. That means that I'll either live with Mum and her boyfriend or I'll live with Dad.

All I know is that I hate what's happened and I wish they loved me more than they do. I think I would prefer to live with Dad because I don't want a stepfather.
Your friend, Glen.

Dear Glen,

My sister May goes to a boarding school. Perhaps if you were to get a place there, you wouldn't have to live with your stepfather and you could visit both your parents in the holidays. My Mum has all the details and I know she wouldn't mind sending them to you. I wish there was something I could say or do to make things better.
Your friend always,
George.

After dinner on the Sunday evening, George was washing the dishes. His father was shouting again. George stood at the sink in the little kitchen, mouthing the words his father was hurling at his mother. George had heard them so often that he knew them off by heart. It was the compost heap speech now.

'If Kent is the garden of England, Biggton must be the compost heap!'

George placed the dishcloth on his hand, forming a crude puppet. 'Next he'll go on about the lack of money, the way the house is run and the dump we all live in. Of course, everything is going to be Mum's fault.' He moved the 'puppet's' mouth in time to his father's ranting. There was silence. George picked up two saucepans and held them above the sink. He counted, 'One, two, three – BANG!'

The pans clashed together at the exact moment his father slammed the front door. 'Off he goes to the Sergeants' Mess again, and he'll come back in a mess too!'

When George finished his task, he closed the kitchen curtains and emptied the rubbish bin. He locked the backdoor and then entered the largest room in the house. It was a combined dining and sitting room, with a coal fire and two windows opposite. His mother was sitting in the dark. George turned the lights on and drew the curtains. His heart ached when he saw his mother's red eyes and tear-stained face. Anger welled up inside him, but he said nothing. He thought that it was best to go to his room, leaving his mother to think. He opened the door to the hallway, and was about to climb the stairs, when something caught his eye.

Lying on the doormat was a crumpled piece of paper. George bent down to pick it up. 'It must have fallen out of Dad's pocket.' It was a receipt for 6 model planes, a double-O gauge train set and a set of books. Like a storm, George blew into the living room. 'He sold it! He sold it!'

'What are you talking about, George?'

'He sold it! He sold it!'

'Calm down, son. Take a few deep breaths; breathe slowly. Now, tell me what you are talking about. Try to stay calm.'

George thrust the receipt under his mother's nose.

'Dad... he... sold... the train set – and your books!'

She held out her arms to George. He didn't respond. His mind was working overtime.

Should he say what was on his heart or keep quiet? He took a deep breath. 'I wish you would divorce him!' The words made his tongue taste foul. He regretted them the instant he spoke. It was too late. He knew that once they left his mouth, he could never push them back in. He felt that he deserved a good shouting at. What his mother did instead was much worse. She burst into tears.

'Don't you ever, ever, say that again! Go to your room and don't come out until I say so.'

George sulked on his bed. He didn't realise that his mother was giving both of them time to calm down. Twenty minutes later, she knocked gently on the bedroom door. She entered the room and knelt by the bed. George sat up. Taking his hands softly in hers, and with an equally gentle voice, she told him,

'Many years ago, I promised your father to love, honour and cherish him; to stay with him always, until death parts us. That promise was to love him in the good times and in the bad times. I know that your friend's parents have broken up, but that's because something went wrong.' George frowned. He didn't quite know where this was leading. His mother continued, 'Loving another person means being prepared to be hurt sometimes. Keeping a promise to love someone forever is one of the greatest things a person can do. I made a promise to your father and to God. No matter what happens, I will never break my promise.'

George was crying now. 'But Mum, Dad's so nasty lately. It's… like… he's not my Dad anymore. That business threatening Stipe – Dad would never have done that before. And selling my train set and planes – that's stealing! Dad used to be my best friend, now he's like my worst enemy.'

His mother held him tightly, stroked his head gently and replied, 'He's not your enemy, but in many ways you're right – your father is not himself lately. He's not well, son. He needs our love and patience. He needs you, George. You must help him when it's the right time.'

'What do you mean?'

'You'll know. Come downstairs with me and I'll get you some chocolate biscuits.'

George followed his mother downstairs. He knew that she was correct. He knew that he should try to understand his father, but secretly, he vowed never to forgive him.

Chapter Five

TURNING POINT

George stood shivering outside the main gates of the base. The sky was still dark and rain blew in his face. A heavy metal song bounced around the inside of his head. It had been playing on the radio. As soon as she heard it, George's mother tuned the radio back to Classic FM, asking, 'Who turned the station over?'

She looked at George, who said nothing, but went a little pink in the face. He left home humming the song his mother had called terrible. George disagreed. He thought the words were appropriate for the day. Getting soaked while waiting for the school bus full of hooligans, to attend a school full of thugs was the perfect time to sing, 'I hate Mondays.' George thought that it was okay to imagine punching someone, or swearing at them, or putting them in a building to be blown to bits.

'After all,' he reasoned, 'I'm not actually hurting anyone – not really. I'm not really being violent to Stipe when I'm thinking of shoving his face down a toilet – not really.' He changed the words of the song from 'I hate Mondays' to 'I hate school days and I hate all days. I hate Stenching, I hate Stipe, and I... I... hate... hate... my... big... fat... bully... of... a... Dad!'

The dirty and dented bus eventually arrived. The words 'Luxury coach' were printed on the side. George climbed aboard the single-decker. He moved half-way down and sat in the middle seats. He preferred to sit at the front, but all the best seats had already been taken. Two schools were represented on the coach – George's school and another school in Westhaven. The children from both schools were equally unpleasant. Only a handful of boys from the RAF base joined George on the bus. When the boys in the back of the bus saw George, they started to call him names.

'That's the little brat who gets his daddy to beat up other kids. He's too soft to stand up for himself. Was that a gorilla your dad had in his car, Tweedie?'

'Do you think that if my Dad had a car, I'd be going to school on a dustcart with all the rubbish every day?'

Something nasty plopped on to George's head. It was spittle. The boy immediately behind him was grinning and looking out of the window. George wiped off the spittle with a tissue. There was another plop. He wiped that off too. There was another plop, then another. The boy behind him had no warning. George pounced upon him, his fists a blur, hammering the boy like piston engines. After the first shock of seeing George leap over the seat had vanished, the boys cheered.

They made so much noise that the driver stopped the coach. George didn't even know the boy who was his punch bag – he'd just had enough. A huge hand grabbed hold of George's collar. He was prised away, his fists still flaying at the air. It was the sight of the bloody face of the boy that made him stop.

The driver roared, 'QUIET!' Silence fell. 'Who started this?' All fingers pointed at George.

'He did!'

'No, I didn't! They spat at me!'

'Shut your fat ugly mouth!' growled the driver. He pushed George to the front of the coach and slung him into the empty seat next to him.

'Stay there! I don't want no more trouble out of you!'
George's eyes bored into the driver. *One more bully to add to my list*, he thought.

For the remainder of the journey, in his imagination he saw a Harrier Jump Jet firing missiles at the bus driver. Before George got off the coach, the driver pointed a thick finger towards him. 'No more trouble from you, sonny, or you'll be walking home tonight. Now clear off!'

You wouldn't dare, he thought. *Anyway, I wouldn't care if you did!*

Morning assemblies at Dunhill were so boring the boys plodded into the hall. As George entered, his attention was drawn to a visitor sitting on the stage next to the head teacher. The visitor fumbled in his pocket and produced a boiled sweet which he popped into his mouth. The head teacher, Mr Mole, stood up and wiped his sweaty brow with a handkerchief. 'Good morning, boys.' He put the cloth back into his pocket. 'I am very pleased to introduce a local celebrity.'

There was a buzz of excitement. The Head raised his hand for silence. It eventually came. 'We are very honoured to have a distinguished guest with us today. It is a privilege to be on the same stage as this great author.' He smiled broadly at the visitor, who gave a little bow in reply. Mr Mole continued, 'I have the great pleasure in introducing Mr Sonnet, the celebrated chairman of the local literary club. He has written many books of poetry and his latest book, 'The Lilies of the Field,' was published last week. Mr Sonnet has taken time out of his busy schedule to visit us this morning, and read poems from his splendid book.' The hall filled with groans. 'Now, now, boys, we'll have none of that.' Discipline threatened to break down completely. Then Mr Stenching stood up. There was instant silence.

'That's better,' said the Head. 'I want you to put your hands together and welcome our guest.' There was a feeble round of applause for the visitor, who changed places with the Head Teacher.

'Thank you very much, Headmaster. The honour is all mine. I am so thrilled to be able to share my complex poetry with your boys. You are a bright bunch of lads but just in case anyone does not understand the meaning of my poetry, I will explain the message contained in each poem after I have read it to you. My first piece is entitled, 'Buttercup' and I wrote it on a summer's day when –'

He spluttered. Went red in the face and grasped his throat. He was choking on the sweet he had obviously forgotten was in his mouth. He spun around to face Mr Mole and coughed. At bullet speed, the sweet flew out of his mouth and bounced off Mr Mole's bald head.

The room was in an uproar. Boys were doubled up, clutching their sides. Teachers rushed to the visitor's aid. It was the shortest assembly ever, and one the boys would never forget. Laughter echoed down the corridors as they went to their lessons.

George still had a smile on his face when he entered room nine with the rest of his English group. Stipe kept his distance from George. As usual, the teacher was late, and Stipe took the opportunity to torment someone. George was not his only victim.   There was a chubby boy called Davis, who had a terrible stammer.

Davis was looking at the tropical fish in the tank at the front of the room. Stipe and two other boys approached Davis.

'Wh… wh… what are y… y… you l… l… looking at D…Davis?'
George clenched his fists around the book he was trying to read. He watched Stipe in disgust.

'What was that? F… f… f… ish!' Cruel laughter slithered out of the mouths of the bullies. Davis backed into the side of the tank.

'L… leave m… m… me alone.'

'W… what d… d… did y… y… you s… s… say?' mocked Stipe.
George stood up. 'You heard him!'

Stipe twisted round. All colour drained from his face –

he couldn't believe his eyes. George was standing with fists at the ready.

'Sit down, Tweedie. This is none of your business.'

'No, I won't sit down, Stipe. I've had enough of you. Now leave him alone.'

Stipe was in turmoil. He wanted nothing more than to engage George in a fight, but the memory of Corporal Scrum was still fresh in his mind. George moved closer. Stipe took a step towards Davis. Davis lost his footing and fell against the fish tank. It exploded on to the floor. Everyone froze. The fish writhed in the splinters of glass.

The door of the room opened. A tall dark-skinned man filled the doorway. All the boys, except George and Davis, rushed back to their seats. George was helping Davis place the fish in the corner sink. The teacher took in the scene and demanded to know what had happened. There was babble as all the boys spoke at once. The teacher's presence was powerful. A raised hand silenced them all.

'One at a time, please – you can tell me what happened,' he said, pointing at Stipe, who smirked at Davis. George stopped Davis from raising his hand and jumped to his feet, placing himself directly in front of the teacher.

'I knocked the tank down, sir. I was messing about and bumped into it. Davis here was good enough to help me try and save the fish. No one else had anything to do with it.'

Astonished faces gawped at George. Why he would take the blame for what his enemy did was a total puzzle. It was also a mystery to George, who was as surprised by his reaction as everyone else. The teacher placed a large hand on George's shoulder.

'Thank you, George Tweedie. Your courage and honesty has saved us all a lot of trouble. You will go to the caretaker and ask him to clear up this mess for us. Then I want you to spend the rest of the period, including break time, in the library. I will give you some work to do for me there.'

George did as he was told. After telling the caretaker about the fish tank, he headed for the library. It suddenly dawned on him that this was more of a reward than a punishment. Being in the library all morning meant being free of his persecutors. George spoke to the librarian, who said abruptly,

'Ah, there you are, Tweedie. Mr Mayflower has left work for you on that desk. Don't disturb the other boys.'

'Thank you, Miss. Er... Miss. Who is Mr Mayflower? I haven't seen him in school before.'

'He is one of the supply teachers.' She frowned.

'What's the matter?'

'Oh, nothing. I thought it was odd that he knew your name, because he only came to the school this morning.'

'Oh.' George had a startling thought. 'When did he put the work on the desk, Miss?'

She bit on the end of a pen, 'First thing after assembly – now get on with your work, there's a good boy.'

George's mind ached in confusion. Mr Mayflower had placed the work in the library *before* the incident with the fish tank. On the desk were a pen, a writing pad and a thin book. A piece of notepaper was attached to the book. The message read: *Read the poem and copy it out. Well done, George. That was a very brave and unselfish thing to do. You are ready to hear about The Song.*

His hands were shaking. He peeled away the notepaper. The title of the book was, 'The Song of the Seraphim.' George shook his head.

He hadn't recognised Mr Mayflower at first, but now he was sure he was the stranger who kept appearing to him in a crisis. George opened the book. There was a single cryptic poem.

In the City of Melodious the Seraphim sing
A song from time's dawn.
The Song in praise of the King.
No heart that is proud can understand the words,
Only in the Golden City can The Song be truly heard.

Throughout eternity the Seraphim call,
They offer their challenge to enter, for all.
Those who pass through the gates of fire
Are welcome and able to hear the Seraphim choir.

George didn't get time to copy the poem, or work out its meaning. He was interrupted by a quiet voice saying, 'Tweedledum, stand up boy.' Mr Stenching's face was like a calm sea. 'You will be sorry to hear that the fish have died. I have spent many years breeding them but it took you only seconds to destroy them.'

George's heart sank to his shoes. Why did the tank have to belong to Stenching of all people? The teacher smiled pleasantly, but his icy eyes made George shiver. He whispered into George's ear, 'How fortunate you are that the law does not allow me to beat you with a cane.' He dug his hand into George's shoulder, and led him out of the library, much to the librarian's annoyance. 'However,' added Mr Stenching, as he led George down the corridor and into the gym, 'there is nothing in the rules about giving you an extra PE lesson.'

'But, sir, I don't have my kit with me. Our PE is normally on a Wednesday.'

'That doesn't matter. You will do the exercises in your underwear.'

George went white with horror at the humiliation of doing exercises in front of the older boys who were using the gym. They sniggered as George undressed to his vest and boxer shorts. Mr Stenching said loudly, 'You wear a vest! You must be the only boy in the 21st century to wear one. Does your mummy make you wear it? Well, answer me, boy.'

'Y... yes, sir.' The gym filled with mocking laughter.

'Now, Tweedledum, I'll knock that pride out of you with a good workout and after lunch you will stand outside my office for the rest of the day.' George went over to his crumpled trousers on the floor and rummaged in the pockets. Mr Stenching asked, 'What are you looking for?'

'My asthma inhaler, Sir'.

'You don't need your inhaler. Give it to me – no do not take it. Give it to me now!' Mr Stenching held out an open palm and George reluctantly placed the inhaler into it. He watched dumbly as an iron fist closed round his precious medicine. All the energy drained out of him.

He was made to climb up and down a rope until his hands burned, then made to run on the spot for thirty minutes. He managed only five, because the pain in his chest forced him to double up. Strange wheezing sounds were coming from his chest and he coughed uncontrollably, gasping for breath.

Mr Stenching made two of the boys carry George to the school office, where he stayed for the rest of the day, under the care of the school secretary, who took George's spare inhaler out of her desk and held him up as he inhaled several puffs. She prevented Mr Stenching from forcing George to stand outside his office in the afternoon.

Mr Stenching bent down to George and hissed in his ear, 'I am not finished with you, boy – you will pay for that fish tank, one way or another.' George sat helpless in a chair, but he silently vowed to make Mr Stenching pay for what he had done to him.

At last the school day ended. George was still weak when he started to board the bus. He felt a tap on his back. It was Stipe.

'Yes?' demanded George.

Stipe was having difficulty in forming the words. George waited for the insult. It never came. Stipe held out a sweaty hand. 'Thanks.' He smiled at George. 'I've told the others from our school to leave you alone on the way home. And, for what it's worth – Stenching was out of order.'

George was dumbstruck. He shook Stipe's hand and boarded the bus. The other boys from Dunhill did leave him alone, but the boy from Westhaven, whom George had beaten up in the morning, desired revenge. He sat behind George. He waited for the bus to be on the country road before he poured manure over George's head. George savaged him – he squealed like a pig. The bus stopped. The driver yanked George off the boy.

'You again! I told you this morning what would happen.' He dragged George to the door and flicked a switch. George was hurled out of the bus.
His bag and overcoat followed. Some of the boys cheered as the bus roared into life and sped away.

George took in his surroundings. He had not noticed, while on the bus, that the forest road was hilly with many twists and bends. Yellow leaves littered the roadside. The trees were stark and hideous in the descending gloom of a winter's evening. George brushed as much muck off himself as he could. He put on the overcoat and slung the bag over his shoulder. He crossed the road to walk on the right-hand side. His father had told him once that, when walking on a country road without a path, you should always face the on-coming traffic.

As he trudged upward, with the wind blowing in his face, George thought how mixed-up his father was. One minute he would be thoughtful and kind, and the next minute, he would be the exact opposite. Only that morning he had yelled at George about something, but had given him some money in case he needed it.

'Use this for a phone box, George, just in case there's a problem.'

'Well… there's a problem now,' panted George, his legs getting heavier by the second. 'But… there's… no… phone box in sight.' The searing pain in his chest made him stop. His ribs felt as if they'd been kicked repeatedly. 'I wish… Mum… and… Dad… could afford to buy me a mobile phone.' George took his inhaler and after a few minutes, his breathing became normal again.

The wind made him shiver. It began to rain. The shadows increased. A car passed him. In the flicker of light, he fancied that he saw something among the trees. A sense of unease, that someone, or something, was watching him, grew in his mind.

Every now and then, a twig would snap and George would stop and turn to face the forest but all he could see were shadows. Another car approached, with its lights on full beam and for a second, eerie sparkling eyes were reflected back from the forest. It was dark again. Terror rose in him and gave him strength to run, but his legs soon turned to jelly. He felt like a vice was squeezing his chest. His lungs felt like a punctured tyre. His breath came in short gasps and his heart beat so fast and so hard that the pounding of his pulse filled his ears.

Water dripped from his brow. His vision blurred. Everything became a hazy mist. He couldn't make sense of the trees, the road or the sky. He ran in slow motion. Invisible weights pulled on his legs. He panted for air. Every breath was a dagger, its pain stabbing through him. His mind pushed him to carry on. *Don't stop now. Keep going. Don't stop.* But he couldn't breathe. The inhaler was useless.

George crossed the road. He had just managed to get to the other side when he fell exhausted against a tree. He forced his body to sit upright and faced the road. At least he would be able to see anything coming out of the forest. Whatever was stalking him would have to cross over too.

It never occurred to George that whatever it was might have already crossed over – not until he could hear the unmistakable noise of crunching twigs behind him. Something was coming closer. He couldn't move. He was too weak. His eyes were lead weights. Something was right behind him. His eyes closed against his will.

He had no idea how long they were shut. When he opened them again, he saw nothing. He was in total darkness. He had the strange feeling that he was floating. At first, he thought that he must be in the boot of a car. Then he realised that he was inside a sack, being carried through the forest. He could hear the crunch of leaves and twigs and muffled voices. They were cruel, angry voices. Now George was certain that he had been kidnapped.

Chapter Six

THE ASEBEIAN

George made a useless effort to free himself from the confines of the sack. Something hard fell against his back.

'Stop that!' shouted an angry voice.

'Keep still you little brat,' hissed another, and then a third, more refined voice spoke. It was calm and superior. George thought it was 'posh.'

'I say, in there,' George felt a huge finger prodding him. 'There's no use in struggling and you needn't be afraid. We are going to stop soon and give you some lovely food to eat.'

'Yeah, nice grub, so shut yer mouth!'

The bag swung violently from side to side. They were evidently travelling at some speed. George's chest was sore from the recent asthma attack. Despite this, his breathing had improved, due mainly to the sleep in the sack.

To take his mind off the growing nausea created by the motion of the sack, George listened carefully to the voices of his captors. He heard four distinct voices. They were young men who argued all the time. He realised that there was a fifth, silent member, because the others referred to him occasionally. The name of the quiet one was Spook.

A miserable voice was complaining. 'Why can't we stop now? I'm hungry and I'm tired of carrying this sack. It's heavy and my arm is aching and my feet are sore.'

'Oh shut yer moaning, Whinger.'

That one speaking now is Grudge. George memorised the strange nicknames. *There's Bile, Whinger, Grudge and Sneaky – I think he must be in charge; he does most of the talking; then there's Spook.* George shivered. He didn't like the sound of him at all. The voices were squabbling about who the leader was. They concluded that all five of them were in charge, and so the bickering continued. *I wish they'd stop arguing. This bag's swinging hard enough as it is.* George's tummy twisted and churned within him. 'I'm going to be sick,' he cried out loud.

'Be sick, then!' grunted Bile.

'I'd love you to be covered in your own vomit,' jeered Grudge.

'But,' moaned Whinger, 'that means I'll 'ave to clean the sick off 'im.'

'You are quite correct, Whinger,' reasoned Sneaky. 'We should stop and give the lad some fresh air. It will do him the world of good. After all, we do want to keep him alive, don't we?'

Spook whispered close to George's ear, 'Alive, yesss, but not for long.'

Without warning, the sack thudded to the ground. George scrambled free and threw up. There was a chorus of cruel laughter. George didn't care. He was glad to be out in the open. He took deep gulps of fresh air, looked up and then his jaw dropped – his captors weren't men – they were giants! Before he could stand up, they clasped chains to his wrists and ankles.

'We don't want yer to run away, now do we?' said Grudge.

'Tie him to a tree and leave him to be eaten by wolvesss,' hissed Spook.

'Do not listen to him, George.'

56

Sneaky patted George on the head. 'There are no wolves in this forest. You are perfectly safe with us.'

Spook couldn't resist saying, 'There are plenty of wormsss and maggots, though.'

They all sniggered and left George chained to a tree. They told him that they were going to look for food and firewood. George's eyes had become used to the dark when he was in the sack. Even so, he couldn't make out his surroundings properly.

He peered through the naked branches of the trees and saw the crystal clear stars shining above. Suddenly the moon appeared from behind a cloud. Its cold light shimmered above the treetops. It only afforded George enough light to see that he was deep in the forest. He had no idea where he was, nor how long he had been asleep in the sack. Just as his captors returned, the moon darted behind a cloud. The shadows shrouded the bodies of his captors. Their faces were also cloaked in the blanket of night.

Despite their constant bickering, the five giants worked together as a team to build a fire. It was very curious how they moved as one. When one bent down to rub sticks together, the others did the same. Finally, George found the courage to ask them, 'Who are you and where are you taking me?'

'Shut yer mouth, brat!' grumbled Bile, 'We're trying to light the fire.'

There was a spark. Then a crackle, spit, snap, and the twigs burst into welcome flames. George was glad of the warmth blowing his way. His heart missed a beat when Spook said in his hideous loud whisper, 'Sshall we let him ssee what we look like?'

The others nodded. They looked up and the moon popped into view. Its glow combined with the flames to produce an eerie light. Now George could see why his captors worked together as one – they were all joined to the same gigantic body.

Two huge feet supported legs as thick as tree trunks. Over these hung an enormous belly and above this flapped a wobbly chest. The creature's skin was a sickly white and covered in matted grey hair. Its arms were thick with muscles. Its hands could easily grasp the trunk of the biggest tree in the forest. The ogre stepped over the fire with ease and in one bound stood in front of George. It was the size of a house. It bent down so close that George's eyes stung and he coughed at the stench that came from the five mouths. An almost attractive head with bobbing blond hair and a constant smile spoke to George with the politeness of a friendly host.

'Let us introduce me to you. I'm known as Sneaky, though I have to say, that is rather unfair. My proper name is – '

'Get on with it will yer!'

'That is Bile.' The left hand pointed to a ginger-headed face, twisted in anger.

'The ugly one on the end, by our right arm, is Whinger.'

'Don't call me ugly!' moaned a hairless head, which was covered in boils and spots.

Sneaky continued.

'This one next to us, by my left hand, is Grudge.'

George looked at the head that had a cone-shaped nose, a slit for a mouth and wore a pointed beard the same colour as its thin black hair. Grudge grunted angrily at George and roared at Sneaky,

'Get on with it, yer bubble-brain!'

'Oh, do be patient! Now, George, I see that Spook has turned around to give you a nice surprise.'

George looked at the head next to Whinger. It had twisted to face the forest. He went cold and clammy as the skull-like head slowly turned to face him. He shuddered when he realised that its matted hair was crawling with maggots. The lip-less mouth bristled with razor sharp teeth. A thin tongue, resembling a worm, crawled out of the mouth as it opened and closed again without uttering a word. All together the heads announced,

'We is Asebeian – that's wot I is!'

'Ow! My backside's burning!' howled Whinger.

The creature bolted upright and patted its bottom, tearing at its blazing loincloth. It writhed in the mud screeching like a siren. All the time the others screamed in pain, Spook said nothing. His unblinking eyes kept their cold penetrating stare upon George. There was silence when the Asebeian finally put the fire out. Then all the heads sighed with relief.

'I suppose you are hungry, George.' said Sneaky smiling broadly.

'How do you know my name?'

Spook answered.

'We know everything about you, George - everything.'

The right hand wiped Whinger's runny nose.

'I'm hungry. When are we going to get some grub?'

'Oh, do be quiet, Whinger!' snapped Sneaky, 'I asked George if he was hungry – not you! Would you like something to eat, young fellow?'

George nodded. He was starving. The right arm tossed a plastic box at George's feet. George fumbled with the lid, and went green at the sight of worms and maggots squirming in the box. He hurled it at the giant, who cackled as the box bounced off its chest.

'Don't you like wormsss, George?' taunted the vile Spook.

'Of course he doesn't,' chimed Sneaky, 'I say, George, we were only joking. Here's your real food.' The left hand placed another plastic box next to George. He hesitated. Sneaky said, 'Go on – you'll love it.'

'Hurry up, brat!' yelled Bile.

George took the lunch box, shook it, and tried to see inside, before gingerly opening the lid. To his delight, it contained an ice-cold bottle of mineral water and all his favourite cold food.

There was a lump of cheese, crusty wholemeal bread buns, tomatoes, pickled onions and a bag of cheese and onion crisps.

For afters there was half a packet of chocolate digestive biscuits and a carton of smooth creamy yoghurt. George was dumbfounded. They certainly did know a lot about him.

He took the bottle of water and downed half of it before starting on the food. The water refreshed him, but the food, though tasty, left him feeling hungrier than before he had started eating. The Asebeian ate raw meat crawling with insects and drank a barrel of beer. George looked away in disgust. He felt Spook's eyes boring into the back of his head. When it finished eating, Sneaky told George to rest.

'We've got a long walk tomorrow.'

'Where are you taking me?'

'We're taking you to Asebeia, our fair city.'

'You do realise that my parents will be looking for me and they will have the police with them.'

The heads wore the look of silent shock. Then they burst out laughing uncontrollably.

'I say, George. That was a good one.' Sneaky was still giggling, 'You see young fellow, nobody can help you now.'

Whinger yawned, 'I'm tired, so belt up, Sneaky.'

'You can't go to sleep!' snapped Bile; 'you're on watch.'

'Me again! It's not fair! I'm always on watch. I'm tired. Grudge can watch for a change.'

Grudge turned towards Whinger and growled, 'I hate you! Anyway, it's Bile's turn.'

Bile went hot in the face, 'Oh no it's not – it's Sneaky's turn.'

'I say old chaps,' answered Sneaky, 'let's not argue. We do believe it's Whinger's turn tonight.'

All four argued. The left hand formed a fist and punched Whinger on the nose. The right hand picked up a log and bashed the head called Sneaky. Both Grudge and Bile yelled in pain. But George couldn't laugh.

He kept glancing at the persistent stare of Spook, who ended the argument by hissing,

'I'll keep watch.'

For what seemed endless hours, George sat on the ground, chained to a tree, with the most frightening face imaginable staring at him. It never moved. It kept its cruel eyes fixed on George. He felt better when darkness finally gave way to the morning light and a blanket of mist covered the forest, covering Spook's face like a veil.

Spook woke the other heads up and the ogre trudged out of sight. George could hear water trickling onto the ground, and the ogre sighing contentedly. When it came back George was forced to his feet and given a drink. He was allowed to relieve himself behind the tree. The ogre prodded him with a stick.

'Get a move on, brat!' shouted Grudge and Bile.

'Where's my bag and overcoat?'

'Oh, I am sorry George,' replied Sneaky, 'but I am afraid that they were mislaid after we picked you up.'

'Wot he means,' said Grudge, 'is he threw them away – ha, ha!' They all jeered and proceeded to prod and push George in the direction they wanted him to go. Once in a while, they yanked at the chain.

Eventually they came to the edge of the forest. George took in the view. The night before, he had had the feeling that he was no longer in Kent. Now he was certain that he wasn't even in England. They were high up on a hill, overlooking a strange landscape. Hundreds of paths left the forest. They formed a gigantic spider's web of granite, strung over a molten sea of fire, which came from a massive volcano in the middle. The ogre pointed a fat finger and proudly announced,

'Asebeia!'

At the centre of the web crouched the forbidding dark city. It waited, like a ravenous beast, ready to devour its prey. It appeared as if someone had used a giant web-shaped pastry cutter to form a pattern in the mouth of the volcano. The city and its many paths were at the top of deep gorges, which descended into the depths of the earth. George recognised the sight. He whispered to himself,

'This is the city in my nightmares.'

The Asebeian made George rest before the long and difficult journey to the city. The creature gave him some apples, blackberries and cool, refreshing water. George knew that the creature didn't act out of kindness when it gave him food; it merely wanted to avoid carrying him.

As he sat on the grassy bank overlooking the hostile landscape, George had time to observe the strange ogre calling itself an Asebeian. He was both fascinated and repulsed by it. He watched with disgust as each head tucked into another meal of raw meat washed down by beer. Where it got the food from was a mystery.

In another time or place, he would have found the creature very amusing. It was quite ridiculous; sitting there with a giant whose five heads squabbled all the time. Occasionally, the arguments ended in a fight. The right arm seemed to be controlled by Whinger, Bile and Spook, while the left arm was controlled by Sneaky and Grudge. The moments when it writhed on the ground punching itself were the most comical. They also afforded an opportunity for escape. However, the instant George thought of running away, the creature became alert and fixed its attention upon its captive.

George learnt to mistrust everything Sneaky said to him. He learnt that Sneaky had stolen his belongings, including the money his father had given him. Yet Sneaky never ceased telling George that he was his friend. George was reminded of something that his father had once told him.

'Never trust someone who smiles all the time, George, and showers you with compliments. Those types are called flatterers. Flattery is when a person hides sinister motives behind a happy face. Do not trust anything they say. Weigh it against the things they do and how they behave.'

George heeded his father's advice and didn't listen to Sneaky.

He did his best to wake up from the nightmare. He pinched himself, slapped his own face, splashed water over his head and shouted,

'Wake up George – you're sitting by a tree on the road – wake up! Oh, why can't I wake up?'

'Because you're not asssleep,' hissed Spook. 'You will be our ssslave until the day you die!'

Chapter Seven

ASEBEIA

Every time George fell, he grazed his knees and enlarged the holes in his trousers. He got no sympathy from the Asebeian when he stumbled on the rocky path. The creature walked in front of him, taking huge strides in its eagerness to reach home. It was impossible for George to keep up without breaking into a run, and that was something his chest didn't want him to do. Every time George slowed down, he fell and was dragged along by the chain.

'Hey!' he yelled. 'Slow down, or carry me!'

'We don't want to carry 'im,' moaned Whinger, 'I want to get 'ome!'

After another argument, it was decided that George should be carried after all. The creature lifted George without any effort. It twirled the chain around its finger and dangled George as if he were a key fob.

Before the journey resumed, Spook whispered something to the others. Deliberately, the right arm holding George moved over the side of the path. An intense heat enveloped him. He looked down at the sea of molten lava spewing from caverns far below. The arm swung over to the other side to reveal the same white-hot sea.

For a few seconds, George was swung from side to side, while the heads giggled with glee. Finally, he was suspended over the right-hand side. The depth of the gorge made George dizzy. Suddenly, the grip on the chain slackened. George's feet began to smoke and his head thumped with the heat. Menacingly, Spook threatened,

'All I have to do isss sssnap the chain and you'll be roasssted alive.'

'Oh do let's get on,' said Sneaky, 'Leave the poor chap alone, Spook – he's frightened enough as it is. Don't worry, George, I'll look after you.' The arm swung away from the molten sea and the chain was twisted around the index finger once more.

It was nightfall when they reached the gate of the city. It resembled a huge mouth cut into the wall. The portcullis was shaped like teeth, which threatened to descend upon George as he was carried through. The gate thudded shut behind them. The creature stopped to gaze lovingly at the city.

'Look, George,' gushed Sneaky, 'this is your new home.' He paused, smiling broadly at the view. 'Isn't it wonderful? Just look at those crystal pyramids, the enormous tower blocks and the wonderful factories. Doesn't the smoke make the chimneys look pretty?'

'No it doesn't! You make it sound like a fun-fair.'

'Oh, this is far better than a fun-fair. You will never get bored here.' The other heads sniggered, but Whinger still managed to complain, 'Oh, get a move on! My feet are killing me.'

'So are mine, dear boy,' replied Sneaky giggling, 'so are mine.'

Regardless of Whinger's protests, George was given a tour of the city. When George had been approaching Asebeia, he thought it looked like a giant hand rising upwards and clawing at the sky. Now he felt suffocated by a dense black forest of dirty tower blocks and chimneys. Buildings of all shapes and sizes stretched for mile upon mile.

The pyramid-like towers were made of smoky crystal. Other towers were made out of stone. Some were round, like the turrets on a castle; others reminded George of ruined skyscrapers. Black and yellow smoke hung in the air. The streets were littered with rubbish and stinking sewage. George's ears were battered by incessant noise; the most irritating noise was a high pitched whistle, which sounded like the whine of a dentist's drill.

Cold air blew soot into George's face and he had a coughing fit. The Asebeian gave him his blue inhaler. 'Where did you get that from? And... why... are you giving it to me?'

'We found this when we picked you up,' said Sneaky, 'and you are going to need it here – we don't want you dying on us – not yet anyway. Now, as I was saying, before you interrupted me with your coughing – which of course you couldn't help, but do try to control it from now on – if you look over there you'll see the m-'

'We'll 'ave to show 'im the mines tomorrow,' grumbled Bile, 'I'm starving hungry.'
George shuddered at the mention of mines.

He was taken to what the Asebeian called a hotel, but it had bars on every window and a steel door on every room. George was flung into a damp hole of a cell. The chain was fastened to the cold wall. 'You will be comfortable here,' explained Sneaky, 'there's food by your feet and water in a bucket.'

'Don't pee in the bucket unless you want to drink it,' Bile added.

'Why did yer tell 'im that?' snapped Grudge, poking Bile in the nose.

'Can we go now?' moaned Whinger, 'I'm hungry, too, and I want to sleep!'

As the creature opened the steel door to leave, Spook turned around to face George. 'It'sss nice and dark in here, George. Don't worry though, there are lotsss of worms and maggotsss to keep you company.'

Bile, Grudge and Whinger laughed, but Sneaky said,

'Leave the boy alone. Don't worry George, the maggots won't hurt you.'

'Oh, please can we go now?' pleaded Whinger.

As the door slammed shut, the room was plunged into darkness. The lock clicked loudly.

George waited for his eyes to adjust to the darkness and was glad of a dim light that came through the bars in the window. A plate, with a metal bowl placed over it, lay to George's right. He touched the bowl and immediately withdrew his hand. It was burning hot. He carefully removed the lid and was surprised to find a knife and fork, wrapped in a napkin, next to the plate. On the plate was a meal of roast beef, roast potatoes, Yorkshire pudding with vegetables and onion gravy. His mouth watered at the sight of this, another of his favourite meals. In his hunger, he soon polished the plate clean.

'Funny, I didn't notice that before.' There was a cup on the floor and next to this a bowl of treacle sponge and custard. The pudding was gorgeous and the water refreshing. The meal had the same effect as the one the previous evening. It looked and tasted good, but gave no nourishment at all. Only the water refreshed him.

The sense of dread never left him. He drifted off into an uneasy sleep, waking up several times during the night. Every time he woke, he was disappointed that he was not in his own bed at home. In the morning he was given another favourite meal, but that too left him feeling hungry and unsatisfied. This was true of every meal in Asebeia; without the water he would die within days.

The days were long and tedious. He was forced to hack away at rocks under the earth. Sometimes he was made to gouge out dirt with his bare hands. There was no reason for the work. It was mindless and without purpose. Sometimes he dug for coal or sulphur to fuel the fires. At other times he helped to make chains – the only product of the factories. Asebeia was a vast prison, a city of slaves, ruled by creatures similar to the one that had captured George.

It was strange to see the streets filled with Asebeians greeting each other cheerily. Each Asebeian was in charge of some wretched person bound in chains. Some were the same age as George. Others were old and frail. After a few days, George was allowed to eat his meals with the other slaves. They met in a dingy hall, furnished with large tables laden with fine food.

He was shocked on his first visit to the dining hall. Nothing could have prepared him for the sight of hundreds of skinny people stuffing food into their mouths. Their bodies were wasted with hunger and hard toil. Whenever a bony hand touched his, George recoiled in horror.

He happened to meet an old man who seemed familiar though he didn't know why. The man's eyes were sunk into his skull. His skin was tight around the bones. They stuck out, making him look like a skeleton with a covering of dirty flesh. His unshaved face bore whitish bristles and his eyes were sad and distant.

'Hello', said George. The man stared blankly at him. *I bet I end up looking like him*! He shuddered at the thought.

No matter how much anyone ate, they never put on any weight. The slaves had no idea how poor and wretched they really were. They believed the food was nourishing. They believed that they were healthy. Some even complained of being overweight. George hoped that he would not become so deceived, so at every mealtime he told himself that he wasn't eating anything at all. He knew that he needed to drink plenty of water to stay alive. Whenever he could, he encouraged other slaves to drink more water. For his efforts, he was made to eat alone in his cell.

George vowed that he would never again complain that something he didn't want to do was boring – not after experiencing the unbroken boredom of slavery in Asebeia. Every day began and ended exactly the same. He was given his food in his cell, led out only to work in the mines. Then he was made to work on a conveyer belt, linking chains.

Later he was given tea; after this, he was made to carry heavy boxes up a flight of stairs in one of the tower blocks. After a day of hard labour, he was chained to the wall of his cell. Even the Asebeian was stuck in a mindless routine. It had the same arguments every day and made the same threats and promises to George. He lost track of time. Seconds seemed like minutes. Minutes seemed like hours. Hours like days. Days like years. He began to long for something that no human being should ever want – he longed to die.

One day Sneaky looked at him with concern.

'Oh, George, you look depressed!' George stared at the stone floor. Sneaky continued. 'I say, chaps, let's cheer him up.'

'Do we 'ave to?' cried Whinger, 'I want to rest.'

'You've just got up, you lazy ape!' growled Bile.

'Oh, do stop arguing, you two,' pleaded Sneaky, 'we must think about poor George here. I think we should try to cheer him up. Don't you agree, Grudge?'

'No, I don't! Take that, yer twit!' Sneaky was punched in the ear and Whinger yelled out loud.

Bile thundered, 'Well I'm bored making 'im do the same stuff every day – I agree with Sneaky.'

'You do?' Sneaky blushed, 'How nice.'

'Oh, all right then!' hissed Grudge, 'Let's take 'im to the fun palace.'

'It's agreed then!' Sneaky was overjoyed.

'Come on, George, we're going to show you another part of the city. You will love the fun palace. There's an endless amount of things to do. And as a special treat, we'll take your chains off once inside.'

George looked at the beast with sudden interest. Perhaps this was a chance to escape. He was picked up and carried through the stinking streets. Spook whispered into George's ear. 'Don't build up your hopesss, Tweedledum - there's no escape from the palace. There isss only one way in and one way out.' Even so, a spark of hope had been lit in George's heart and he did his best to fan it into flame.

Chapter Eight

THE FUN PALACE

The oval building stood in the oldest part of the city. Crumbling red-brick houses were dotted around it. High above the domed roof flashed a tacky neon sign. Its red and green letters proclaimed 'Fun Palace.' The dirty gold paint was peeling away from the brickwork. Two large glass doors were the only way in and out of the building. The Asebeian let George down onto his feet. He felt dizzy after swinging on his chain, dangled from the end of the creature's finger.

George observed that the wall nearby was neglected. In certain places the bricks were crumbled or had tumbled down. He could easily scramble over part of the wall. All he had to do now was escape from the clutches of the Asebeian.

That was the difficult part. The creature didn't remove the chains until they were inside the building. George was taken along the curved corridor to a single inner door.

Before opening the door, Sneaky beamed at George and enthusiastically told him, 'Now, George, you can do whatever you want to do in here. You'll make new friends and have lots of fun.'

Spook whispered loudly, 'We'll be back in two hoursss.' The door was pushed open and the Asebeian nudged its prisoner through. George was delighted to be free from his slave master, but puzzled by its desire to reward him.

His ears were assaulted by a deafening noise. The high pitched whine that pervaded the city was magnified by the shape of the roof. The building had the design of a concert hall, so all sounds were amplified. Electronic whines, pops, bangs and whistles came from an array of video machines. Pinball tables clanked and rattled. Money clattered out of gambling machines. Banks of television screens lined the walls. Laser guns fired and disco lights swirled in the darkness.

George was disturbed by the sight of hundreds of wiry people mesmerised by a mindless game. He had never had any interest in such things.

However, at the back of the hall, there was something that caught his eye. He walked past everyone with mounting excitement. A smile brightened his face. His pace quickened. He reached a partition. Behind this was the object of his desire. He stood for a moment, gazing in wonder. There, on a raised platform, was a magnificent train set – better than the one his father had made for him. George was captivated by the layout. He picked up the controls and started to play. His surroundings disappeared. The sounds no longer bothered him.

He believed that he was back in his bedroom in Fordale, happy and secure, playing at trains with his father. Left alone in this wonderful illusion, George would have been content to stay in Asebeia for the rest of his life.

When the Asebeian came for him, George begged,

'I want to stay – please can I stay?'

'Not now,' young fellow, said Sneaky, 'but you'll be back, don't worry.'

'When?'

'Very soon, after you've done a little more work in the mines.'

After two days, George was pleading with the Asebeian to go back. It was all he could think of. After begging for a

72

week, the Asebeian took him back. George went every day and began to treat the creature as if it were one of his parents. It would pat him on the head after it removed the chains and George would wave goodbye, before running off to play. Sometimes the Asebeian would stay and play with him, not only with the train set, but also showing him how to play the video games. George was so happy that the months flew by. On the evening of the seventh month, the Asebeian took him back to the cell and as usual George hugged the creature's huge leg.

'Thank you, Asebeian. Can we play on the laser guns tomorrow?'

'We'll see.'

The creature gently brushed George's thinning hair and patted his bony cheeks. All the heads said at once, 'Good night, dear boy.'

'Good night, my friends,' answered George as they attached the chains to him. He waved at the ogre as it closed the door.

George grinned, recalling the fun he had enjoyed that day. Then he stopped grinning as a finger of light cut through the darkness. He bolted upright and the chains rattled. The light grew stronger. He was bathed in a warm glow. A gentle sound washed over him. Music kissed his ears. He had forgotten what music sounded like. Someone from outside the cell was singing a wonderful song. The song was indescribably beautiful. The words were sung in a language George had never heard before, but the tune sounded familiar.

'I've heard this song before, a very long time ago… when though? Come on, George think!' He dug deep into his memory. 'That's it! Mum used to sing it to me when I was about three!' Then he remembered the poem he had read in the school library. 'This must be 'The Song of the Seraphim.' Only in Melodious can the words be understood.' George didn't know where Melodious was. What he did know was that he wanted to be there. He wanted to see the Seraphim and join in with their singing.

The song soothed him so much that he fell into a deep, peaceful sleep. He didn't know when the song ended, but it filled his dreams. Visions of a golden city, beautiful animals and strange flying creatures of fire, flooded his mind.

When he woke in the morning, the melody remained with him. It stayed with him down the mines. It followed him up the stairs of the tower blocks. It accompanied him to the doors of the oval building. As he left the Asebeian, it suddenly occurred to George to wonder who had sung the song the night before. The voice had been so haunting and beautiful, that the hairs on his neck had stood on end. He could have listened to that voice forever and never grown tired of it.

Instead of playing, he wandered about the hall, looking for another exit, which he didn't find. The only exit was the inner door to the corridors. The Asebeian had told George that this was where it and the other Asebeians rested while the slaves played. George carefully opened the door just enough to see the creatures slumped on the floor and in a stupor. They looked like gluttons after too much food. As he watched them he felt drained of energy. Suddenly, he shuddered at the thought that the creatures might be feeding off the energy of the gamers.

He gently closed the door and explored the hall. A gigantic television screen caught George's eye. The people on the TV were familiar to him. As he moved closer for a better look, he was amazed to see himself on the television.

Chapter Nine

BITTER MEMORIES

George watched in fascination as a scene from his past played out before him. He remembered it well, it was the day he turned ten and he remembered feeling bad about having to go to school on his birthday...

He had entered his classroom and said hello to Jessica and Gail, the two girls who sat next to him. He slid open the plastic book tray from under his table. It felt heavy and rather sticky. The contents of the tray were moving! The sight of writhing worms sent George into a panic and he knocked the tray onto the floor. The girls erupted into wild screams. Helen and Harold doubled up in laughter. Miss Jackson entered the scene of confusion. Children were laughing, screaming and darting all over the place. A hundred earthworms were wriggling under the table of George Tweedie. He was the bright green statue doing his best not to be sick.

Miss Jackson was determined that pranks of this nature were not tolerated, so she made George apologise to Jessica and Gail, and then ordered him to pick up the worms. Instead, George ran out of the class and threw up in the boys' toilets. Someone else had to clean up the mess and George spent the first playtime in detention.

Harold Snoad-Tomkinson and Helen Risdale were the school bullies and, as bad luck would have it, both were in George's class. They knew of George's fear of worms. They had sneaked into the classroom, placed the worms in the tray and run off to tell Miss Jackson that George was about to play a trick on the girls who sat at his table. It was no use George protesting his innocence. He knew from experience that the bullies had a way of making him appear to be the culprit and not the victim.

On the screen, George saw himself in the playground surrounded by Helen, Harold and the gang who hung around the two bullies like faithful puppy dogs.

'Like my birthday present?' asked Harold mockingly. 'Was the little baby sick at the sight of the little worms?'

George's stomach felt like a sack of potatoes, his legs were like lead weights and his skin went cold with fear. His mind told him that if he stood up to them, they would probably back away. But his feelings confused his mind because he had been bullied for years and he accepted the insults slung at him as a fact of life. It was a cruel coincidence that not only did he share the same classroom as Helen and Harold; he also shared the same birthday.

Harold asked George, 'What else did you get for your birthday?'

George didn't answer but Harold goaded him until he said. 'I got a model train for my set.'

'A model train! Is that all? I got an iPad!'

'So did I!' exclaimed Helen; 'I also got a pony! And I got perfume and clothes and my Daddy's taking me to Switzerland for a skiing holiday!'

'My Dad's giving me a lesson in a glider!' Harold pushed George. 'That's far better than playing with a little model train.'

George was furious, but didn't know what to say.

'Of course, George,' Helen wore an understanding expression, 'we do understand that your poor parents can't afford to buy you decent presents. What does your father do? Ah yes! He's a cook isn't he?'

'He's a chef – not a cook!' George bit his lip, knowing that he'd just given her reason to continue. 'I am terribly sorry,' she said, shaking her head. 'He's only a chef and don't forget he's a sergeant too; whereas my Daddy's a captain and a pilot.'

'So what?'

'So what? Well... my Daddy can fly a fighter jet, what does your father fly – a pancake?'

There was a peal of laughter. George tried to act as if he didn't care, but his red face betrayed his feelings. Harold saw that the goading was having the desired effect, so he asked George if his father ever went on active duty, joining other forces in a war zone. George knew that the best defence was to say nothing and walk away, but both his arms were being squeezed tightly by two of the bullies, making it impossible for him to break free.

He was too wound up to stay quiet. He snapped at Harold saying, 'Yes he does go on active duty!'

'I just wondered,' mused Harold. 'Will he be cooking or fighting?'

'Both. He told me that on active duty he's a soldier first and a chef second. He's been trained to fight and he's an A1 marksman. I've seen him practise with an air gun and he hits the bull's-eye every time.'

'What does your father use for ammo?'

'Bullets of course.'

George silently rebuked himself when he realised that he had fallen into Harold's trap. The spiteful boy sneered.

'I just wondered, because I've seen your father load his gun with hard peas!' The mocking laughter grated in George's ears while Harold continued his taunting. 'That's what your father does; he fires his rotten cooking at the enemy. Instead of torpedoes he uses sausages!'

'And rock cakes instead of hand-grenades!' added Helen.

This opened a floodgate of suggestions of what George's father could use as ammunition, which ranged from cold porridge to things far cruder. George could not

77

stand the insults anymore. His rage bubbled to the surface and he pounced on his tormentors like a demented Rottweiler. Mr Solomon, the head teacher arrived, pulled George off Harold, who was screaming with fear, and promptly punished George...

'No! That's not what happened!' said George to the television. 'I remember it differently – Glen was there – he stuck up for me. I didn't fight, though I wanted to. Mr Solomon came just when I was about to hit Harold. Mr Solomon punished the bullies, not me.' The scene changed again. It was the evening of his birthday...

The guests were due to arrive for the party, but no-one came. Glen wasn't able to come; it was that night his parents told him that they were moving to Germany. George's mother telephoned the parents of the children who had accepted invitations to the party. Some of the parents made excuses, saying that they had got the dates mixed up and their children were unable to come. Most of the parents were surprised to hear that their children were not at the party. Further investigations revealed that the children had gone to the other party being held on the base that night. George sat in an increasingly gloomy mood, hearing that his so-called friends had gone to the party organised by Helen. She had persuaded her parents to hold a joint party for herself and Harold. George ran up to his room, 'Everyone hates me!' he moaned, as he slumped onto his bed and tried to fight back the tears...

The memories on the screen were bitter and George could have easily wallowed in self-pity, but the beautiful tune trickling back into his mind helped him to remember that it wasn't all bad. His family had made the party very special by showing him how much they loved him. He could remember the delicious smell of freshly baked cakes, the wonderful presents and the way his family treated him as if he were a king.

George looked away from the television as it began to show the scene when his father had to leave for the war in the Middle East. He didn't want to watch anymore. He knew that the memories weren't completely true because they only showed the bad bits.

George decided to speak to the others in the hall. All of them were trapped in their own little worlds. He spied a familiar girl's face. She was lost in a video game. George was shocked when he saw her. He said her name, but the girl ignored him and carried on playing. He grabbed hold of her and turned the stool she was sitting on around to face him. He looked into her eyes.

'May! May! How long have you been here?'

'Who are you?'

'It's me, George – your brother.'

She stared at him blankly. Slowly, she recognised him.

'Oh hello, George.' Her face remained vacant as she said, 'Oh George, isn't it great here! Look! I'm on level ninety five!' She spun back to the screen.

'May, we've got to get out of here.'

'Don't talk rubbish! It's wonderful here. Now, be a good boy and leave me alone.'

'May, we're in a big prison on another world... or something like that.'

'What you on about? We're on holiday at the seaside!'

'No, May, we've got to get out of here.'

'Oh look – you've made me lose a life! Get lost!'

He didn't know what to say, so he left her and explored the rest of the hall. Behind another screen, were vending machines full of sweets, fizzy drinks and alcohol. George looked to see if there was any water hidden among the other drinks, and when he found some, he selected two bottles.

There were tables, near the vending machines, and sitting at one of them was a shrivelled old man staring into his glass of beer. George recognised him as the man he had spoken to in the dining hall when he first arrived in the city.

He approached the table and politely asked,

'Can I join you?'

The old man nodded. His deep, grey eyes were sad and troubled. George shuddered. The man looked like someone who was about to die. He was terribly thin. As George spoke with him, a dim spark of life flashed in the old man's eyes.

'Hello, my name is George. What's your name?'

'What's my what?'

'Your name. What's your name?'

The man shook his head. 'I don't remember.' He brushed his white hair with his twisted hand, 'No-one has asked me for my name for such a long time. Actually, no-one has spoken to me, except the monster that captured me.'

'Well, I'm speaking to you now.' George smiled.

The old man was startled. He hadn't seen a smile for so long. He tried to smile, but the muscles on his face wouldn't let him. Yet a sparkle filled his eyes.

'Thank you,' he said, 'you are kind.'

'I know, I'll give you a name. Would you like that?'

The man nodded in reply, 'I would like that very much.'

'Let's see.' George rubbed his chin thoughtfully. 'I know! I'll call you Pops – you remind me of my granddad.'

'That sounds good. I... I... think... I... had children once. I can't remember... But you don't want to talk to me, young man. I'm a bad person.'

'I don't believe that. You don't look as if you belong here at all.'

George fell silent. He looked across to May. He wished that he had managed to get through to her. Perhaps he could help the old man. Turning back to his new companion, George asked him if he wanted another drink. He went back to the vending machine and returned with another can of beer and a bottle of water. The old man thanked him and emptied half the can.

'I never used to drink this much before.'

'Why do you drink a lot now?'

'I want to forget.'

'Forget what, Pops?'

The old man's face writhed in agony. He grasped George's hand.

'You must leave me, boy! I've done terrible things – terrible things!'

George was a little frightened. Nevertheless, he persisted in trying to help the troubled man. 'Listen!' he said with authority, 'I'm not leaving you until you give me a good reason.'

'Why are you bothering? You will leave me when you know what I've done.'

'What have you done?'

'Terrible things, boy - evil things.'

George was uneasy. What if he were talking with a murderer? He shook the thought out of his head.

'Tell me what you've done.'

The old man sighed deeply.

'I was a witness to things no human should ever see. Evil things… I can't tell you what they were. They're too horrible to mention.' He suddenly gripped George's shoulders.

His face was twisted in pain – the eyes stared wildly beyond George to some horror he had witnessed. 'There was fighting, killing, cutting, shooting…'

George didn't recoil from the grip. Tears rolled down his cheeks. He gently squeezed the man's gnarled hand. Softly, he said,

'Sounds like you were in a war.'

'Yes! That's it! I was in a war… a terrible, unnecessary war.'

'Then you aren't to blame.'

'You think so?'

'Yes I do. War is horrible. I've seen war films where men were ruined by being in awful battles.'

'But… I… killed someone. I shot another human being!'

'Did you want to kill them?'

The old man took a sip of beer. He shook his head,

'No, I don't think I did. There were many soldiers in the tent. A man came in… he had a machine gun… he shot many of my friends. I tried to stop him… I shot him. I murdered him!'

George struggled for the right words,

'I don't think you meant to kill him. It sounds as if you saved many lives.'

Tears ran down the old man's crumpled face.

'No – I killed someone.'

'I believe that you're really a kind man and you didn't mean to kill. You were forced to do something terrible and you hate what you've done.'

George glanced around him.

'Listen, I heard this song last night.'

'What's a song?'

'It's music.'

The old man frowned.

'What on earth is music?'

George repeated something his mother had once told him.

'Music is the language of the soul. Without it, our lives are empty and without meaning. Music keeps us sane. It has a way of wrapping itself around our emotions and lifts our spirits.'

'I like the sound of that.'

George made a decision. He began to sing the song he had heard in his cell. He sang the words of the poem to the tune. They fitted perfectly.

'In the city of Melodious, the Seraphim sing…'

All the noises in the room stopped. Everyone turned to look at the singer. He felt a powerful grip crush his shoulder. He was lifted violently off the stool. The Asebeian carried him out of the hall. All the heads were shouting abuse at George. 'That sound is not allowed here. You'll rot in the dungeon from now on.'

While the creature tried to fasten the chains to George's

wrists, he struggled in fury. The Asebeian loosened its grip. George broke free and he ran. He darted towards the crumbled part of the wall. The ogre was so startled it tried to run in two directions at once and fell over.

'Come on!' shouted Bile, 'We've got to work together to catch the brat!'

'But he ran to the left!' exclaimed Sneaky.

'No he didn't! He ran to the right – come on you idiot!' It tumbled over again. With the right fist, Bile punched Sneaky in the eye. Spook stopped the argument by hissing,

'Fools! He ran to the wall which is on the left.'

'See, I was right!' snapped Sneaky, 'He ran to the left.'

George had climbed over the wall and was on a path, running towards the forest. Twigs gashed his face. His feet sank into a bog. The more he struggled, the quicker he sank. He heard the Asebeian crash through the trees.

It stood before him and laughed. Spook gloated,

'We told you that there is no escape. Now you will rot in the city. And we'll beat that awful noise out of you.'

The creature lifted George out of the mire with ease. He was taken to the top of one of the round, turret-like towers. Chains were fastened around his neck, arms and legs. The door was bolted and darkness engulfed him.

Chapter Ten

ASTRID

There were no windows in the cell. George sat in total darkness, but eventually his eyes got used to it. He could see everything in a grey mist and make out the bucket of fresh water that was beside him. The Asebeian returned two days later. It loomed over George, acting as if it were a friend who had been betrayed. As usual, Sneaky did most of the speaking.

'Oh, George, how could you? After all the things we've done for you, you repay us by running away. I'm disappointed in you and yet we is willing to give you another chance, if you have learned your lesson.'

George took no notice, until Sneaky said,

'After a week in here, you can return to the Fun Palace, as long as you promise not to make that disagreeable sound.'

George pulled at the chains and shouted,

'I won't promise – I'll sing the song all the time!'

The Asebeian held a leather belt in its left hand. It raised it, while Grudge yelled,

'Don't you dare speak to us like that!' It beat George with the belt. Each head hurled abuse at him.

Suddenly, the Asebeian backed away in alarm. Instead of begging for mercy, George was humming the tune.

Then he shouted in defiance,

'I don't care if you beat me! I will not go back to the Fun Palace. I hate that place! I hate this city! I hate you!'

The creature was at the open door. Spook spat out the words,

'We'll kill you, you little brat. We'll let you die in this prison.'

'Let me die then! I'd rather rot in this hole than serve you!'

Dazed and confused, the Asebeian backed out of the cell, slamming the door behind it. It descended the twisting stairwell. The heads were arguing and trying to decide what to do next. They were completely unprepared for George's resistance.

'I've got a headache,' Whinger moaned.

'So 'ave we,' replied the others. The voices vanished into the distance. Save for the high-pitched whine, all was silent. George slumped into the muck on the cold floor. He was exhausted from the beating. His eyes closed and he fell into a fitful sleep.

In the dead of night, he awoke. His breathing had become laboured and his chest was wheezy. He was too weak to reach the bucket of water, so his mouth remained dusty. The cell door opened silently. A blaze of light banished the darkness. George closed his stinging eyes.

'You can open your eyes now,' said a gentle female voice. When he looked, the light had become warmer and kinder to his eyes.

There was a figure, bathed in a soft glow, standing in the doorway. It was a girl about the same age as George. She wore the typical clothes of an eleven-year-old: Jeans, woollen top and white trainers. She looked Jamaican, yet her skin was light brown rather than ebony. Her long black hair was tied in a ponytail and her eyes sparkled with life. Her beauty was like soothing ointment on George's eyes. It took away the sting of despair. She placed an old-fashioned lantern on the floor and removed a rucksack from her back.

The girl was gently singing the same mysterious song he had heard a few nights before. The light seemed to dance to the tune. It shimmered in the air and formed the shape of a sword. She grasped the sword with both hands. With swift and decisive movements, she sliced through the chains with ease. When the girl stopped singing, the sword vanished.

'Who are you?' whispered George.

In reply, she put a finger to her lips. Kneeling down in front of George, she opened the rucksack and produced a handful of tiny tear-shaped crystals. Holding them flat in her palm, she pursed her lips and gently blew the crystals in George's face. Immediately his breathing eased. The pain left his chest and, within seconds, he was breathing normally.

Next, like an experienced nurse, the girl applied some cream to George's wrists and ankles. The soreness melted away. She rummaged in the sack again and took out a flask. There was a pop as she took off the plastic cup, which she gave to George, and then she poured white liquid into it.

'Drink this slowly. You haven't had proper food for a long time. Be careful though 'cause the milk's hot and it's got spice in it.'

'It's yummy! I feel all warm inside.'

The girl brought out a small loaf of bread.

'Eat this slowly, too.'

George bit into the delicious soft bread and gazed with wonder into the girl's big brown eyes. They were moist with sorrow. She gently brushed his head. The only other person to show him this kind of love was his own mother. The girl sat cross-legged, watching George eat. With each bite and sip he grew stronger, as did the question overwhelming his thoughts. The girl announced,

'Me name is Astrid.' Her tone was light and natural. She had a strong north-eastern accent and spoke as if they were in a playground, not a dungeon.

George replied, 'That's a lovely name.'

'Thanks. Me full name is Astrid Cathryn Charis. Me Dad's from Newcastle-on-Tyne and me Mam's from Jamaica. I'm of mixed race but I'm not mixed up. Oh, and I've got six sisters.'

'Oh,' replied George in a daze. 'This is lovely food, thank you.'

'You're welcome. Want some more?'

'Yes please.'

She handed him another loaf of bread and refilled his cup. In answer to another unspoken question, she said,

'I've been sent by Daionas to lead yer out of the city when yer feel stronger.'

'Oh. What was that stuff you blew in my face? My chest feels great.'

'They're called *The Tears of Daionas*. But yer asthma's not cured. You've just been given relief for a little while.'

'How do you know I've got asthma?'

A mischievous grin filled her face.

'You'd be surprised by what I know.' He looked at her with suspicion. She burst out laughing.

'Oh George, cheer up! I've been sent to help you, not torment you. Mind you, I can understand why you'd be uneasy after being here for so long. How do you feel now?'

'Much better thanks. Who is Daionas?'

'He is the King of Light. He is completely good, with no bad in Him at all. The Seraphim sing about Him all the time and you'll meet Him in Melodious, where He reigns.'

'Oh!' He was quiet for a moment, then asked, 'Was it you who sang that song to me the other night?'

'No, that was our guardian, Luminous. You'll meet him soon enough.'

'How did you get here?' he asked. 'I haven't seen you anywhere in the city before.'

'That's 'cause I don't belong in the city and neither do you. I've been sent by Daionas to help you escape.' She beamed a bright smile at him, then announced:

'I'll be your guide – will you trust me?'

'Yes, I will.'

'Good! Are you strong enough to stand?' She bounced up and held George's arms; unfortunately, he was unable to stand up.

'You poor thing! You're like a skeleton, you know.'

'Am I?' George was surprised, until he remembered how everyone looked in Asebeia. So, despite his best efforts, he too had been deceived into thinking that he was okay.

Astrid held out a piece of strange, reddish fruit. It was three times the size of an apple and tasted like a rich, juicy fruit salad.

'That's a fire berry from the trees in Melodious. It's all your favourite puddings rolled into one. It will take a while to eat because it's so filling. I remember me first fire berry, it was so…' She checked herself. 'I'm babbling. It's a bad habit of mine.'

George munched happily on the gorgeous fruit. He felt the strength return to his legs. He frowned and asked,

'Why have you turned up now and not before – to rescue me I mean?'

'You weren't ready before, but you are now. You see, when you resisted the Asebeian, you proved that you were ready to leave… and ready to hear the truth about yourself. You've done two of the three things needed to leave this place.'

He was about to ask another question when she held up her hand, saying,

'Just listen, while I try to explain. First, you hate this city and all it stands for. You were really taken in by that train set 'til Luminous sang his song to you. The fact that you tried to sing it to others shows that your heart is ready. Secondly, you resisted the creature. Now you're not its slave. It's very important not to give in to it, or you will make it strong.'

'How?'

'Oh, I forgot – yer don't know what it is yet.'

'I hate it, whatever it is. Er, what is it?'

'It's a reflection of what you're like on the inside. It's all your bad feelings and attitudes made visible. Each head stands for a bad feeling. Just think about the names they call each other. Sneaky is deceit. He's a hypocrite and a liar.'

'I know; he pretends to be my friend when he's really my enemy. And he says one thing, but means something else.'

'That's right. Let's see if you can work out who's who.' She looked thoughtful. 'I know! What do you feel when Spook looks at you?'

George shuddered, 'Terrified.'

'Okay, so what's he stand for?'

George had finished eating and placed his hands in his lap. He was relaxed and found the idea of a game appealing. It didn't take a genius to answer the question.

'Spook is my fear.'

Astrid clapped her hands together.

'Correct! What about Bile?'

He thought about the way Bile shouted all the time and how he was always in a bad mood.

'He's my anger.'

'Correct again – you're good at this! What about Whinger?'

'Well, he's the ugliest of the lot.' He grinned broadly.

'Oh, I know! He's self-pity!'

'Okay, that brings us to the last and definitely least of all, Grudge.'

George shook his head. Silence followed. He knew what Grudge represented, but he didn't want to admit it.

'Well?' asked Astrid. She knew why George struggled and had been reluctant to challenge him, although she knew she had to.

'I'll give you a clue. A grudge is when you want to get your own back on someone who's upset you or hurt you.'

'I do know… it's my hatred isn't it?' Astrid nodded.

'Yes, and it's your murderous desire for revenge on your enemies and everyone who has ever hurt you.'

'Murderous! I've NEVER wanted to murder anyone!'

'Haven't you?' Astrid did not raise her voice; neither did she condemn George, though she faced him with the awful truth.

'I'd call imagining a Harrier Jump Jet blowing people to bits pretty murderous.' She let the truth sink in. George stared back at her. Astrid took a deep breath,

'This brings me to the third thing you must do if you want to be free from the Asebeian.'

She hesitated. She took hold of his hands, looked him straight in the eyes and said,

'You must forgive the bullies, including the teachers. You must forgive those who haven't helped you... and most of all... you must forgive yer dad.'

'NO!' George shot to his feet. He began to pace the cell.

'No, no, no! I can't do that! They've made my life a misery and all because I'm different somehow. The new boy – the RAF kid! I can't forgive. I won't forgive!'

Astrid was wearing the rucksack again in readiness to leave. She had been warned that George would react in this way.

'George, I know all about being picked on because of being different. Look at me – I'm black – think of the names I get called. I know it's hard, but yer must forgive them, especially yer dad.'

'No! He hurts my Mum and he drinks and he took away my train set.'

'A train set is only a thing, George. Yer dad is a person. He's more important than things.' Astrid heard the thud of footsteps on the stairs.

George wallowed in self-pity and shouted; 'You don't understand! I don't have any friends. I've nowhere to go. That train set was like a friend to me. It was a way of escape. It's just not fair! I hate them all!'

The Asebeian stood in the doorway. It looked different. Spook and Sneaky were smaller than Whinger and Bile. Grudge was now the biggest head. The expressions on all the faces were fierce and totally evil, even Sneaky had lost his smile. Grudge demanded,

'Wot's going on? Where did you come from?' The creature squeezed itself into the cell. It kicked the lantern over, smashing it to bits. It raised a club to batter Astrid. George blocked its way. He was knocked to the floor and winded. Astrid shouted,

'LUMINOUS!'

The Asebeian screamed in terror and twisted in pain as an awesome creature of intense light appeared in the cell. It wasn't made of flesh and blood, but was formed from sparking fire. It was like a firework continually exploding in the night sky. The face was overwhelming, with amazing dark eyes. It was a living star, in the pattern of a creature half man, half lion, and it had six mighty wings.

At the sight of the dazzling creature, the Asebeian fled and tumbled down the stairs. All was quiet. The Seraphim transformed into a giant of a man. A man very familiar to George. He was the black American who had come to George's aid on many occasions.

'Hello, George. I have come to help you again.' George was dumbstruck.

Astrid broke the silence. 'Is it dead?'

'No, it is in a deep sleep. Daionas commands you to bring George as he is. I've made it possible for him to resist the Asebeian's influence.'

George finally found his voice.

'Mr Mayflower?'

'That was a name I gave myself once. I am Luminous, one of the Seraphim. I am guardian to both of you.' He bowed low, 'I am here to serve.'

'We must hurry, Luminous, before George is too weak again.' She helped George to his feet.

He was red with shame. 'I'm sorry, Astrid – for blowing up like that.'

'That's okay. Come on – we must hurry. It will be daylight soon and the other Asebeians may try to stop us before we reach the path.'

Luminous touched the wall with the palm of his hand and the stones melted away.

'We cannot use the stairs, because that repulsive creature blocks the way.' Light shone out of him and he returned to the fiery shape of the Seraphim. His face was still recognisable as the man who had stood before them a moment before, and yet his voice sounded like a choir of a thousand singers.

'I will carry you down the tower to the bridge.'

He lifted the children without effort and shot out of the hole in the wall. 'You must cross the bridge yourself, George. It is a test of your decision to trust us.'

George didn't understand what Luminous meant, until he was placed on the ground by a deep chasm. The Seraphim flew away. George wished that he could fly with him.

'Don't worry,' chirped Astrid. 'Luminous will be back if we need him and we can always call for Daionas.' George recognised the deep gorges as the ones he had crossed to enter the city.

He shivered at the memory of the Asebeian dangling him over the edge. He looked down and felt dizzy.

'Astrid?'

'Yes?'

'Er, where's the path across the chasm?'

'It's over there,' she replied lazily, while pointing to a narrow wooden bridge. It was suspended across a raging sea of lava. George gasped in horror.

'We have to cross that! It doesn't look very safe.'

'It's stronger than it looks.'

She faced him and touched his arm. He had gone white as snow.

'You'll be all right, George, I promise you. I'll walk behind you, because we have to cross it in single file.'

'But I'm scared of heights.'

'Want to know a secret?'

'Okay.'

'I'm scared of heights too.'

Her face was aglow with a cheeky grin, 'Actually, that's not quite accurate. What I'm really scared of is falling!' She laughed and George joined in, though he was puzzled.

'Why do we have to use this bridge and not one of the paths?'

'Because there are many ways into the city but only one way out of it – and this is it!'

A gust of wind blew against the bridge. It swayed violently from side to side. The children were half way across the suspension bridge when dawn broke. The sun added its heat to that of the lava below. Astrid kept George's mind off the danger by chatting merrily to him.

They discovered that they had a lot in common. Both liked Science Fiction, so they talked about their favourite books, films and TV programmes. Astrid told George that she loved all kinds of music and that she could play the clarinet.

'I'm also learning to play the drums.'

'That sounds like fun. My school doesn't teach music.'

'That's too bad. I bet you could play an instrument.'

He turned in surprise, still careful to keep a firm grip on the ropes. 'Do you really think so?'

'Yes, I do, and keep your eyes front.'

Sweat was pouring off George. It was clear to Astrid that he was becoming fearful again. He couldn't turn around. 'Keep looking down, George.'

'You must be joking! There's no way I'm going to look down!' He looked straight ahead and walked with fresh determination. Astrid smiled at his back.

George asked her,

'What job has your dad got?' There was an awkward silence. George stopped and faced her. Her expression was painfully sad. 'He was a bus driver, but he died of a sudden heart attack a year ago.'

'I'm sorry – I don't know what to say – it must be awful to lose a parent.' His eyes misted over and he stared into the distance. He felt that he had lost his father too, but instead of feeling angry towards him, there was a longing for them to be friends again.

Astrid touched his hand gently,

'Don't be sorry, George, Daionas will help you as he has helped me. I'll tell you what he did for me some other time, but we must keep moving.'

George resumed crossing the bridge. Looking ahead, he asked Astrid,

'How does your mum manage with seven kids to look after?'

'Well, we've got family living nearby. Me Granny lives with us, and me aunts and uncles help too. Anyway, two of me sisters have left home for university and two are married, so me mam has only me and me sisters Ruth and Jenny to look after.'

'Are you the youngest?'

'Not quite.'

'What do you mean, 'not quite?''

She chuckled. 'Well, me and Jenny are twins.'

'There isn't two of you!'

'Of course not! Me sister may look like me, but she's very different. She's not as...'

'Bubbly?'

'Yeah! Not as bubbly as me.'

George looked down. The lava was spewing up from the chasm below. He was glued to the bridge. He couldn't take his eyes off the river of fire, or move a step in any direction. The heat became overpowering. A spark spat over the bridge. Then another flame shot upwards, followed by a blaze of dazzling sparks bouncing all around them. The bridge began to sway violently. Both turned around, to see the Asebeian hacking at the ropes with an axe.

Chapter Eleven

ZENOBIEL

George was still frozen to the spot, but Astrid remained completely calm.

'George, don't be afraid, just keep going. We're nearly there.'

'The bridge is on fire!'

'No, it's not. It can't be destroyed. Just keep moving.'

'But the ogre – it's cutting the bridge! It's cutting the bridge!'

'Take me hand.' Her voice was quiet and assured.

'Listen to me; it can't cut the rope, because this bridge was built by Daionas Himself. No one can destroy what He's made. It's just trying to frighten you.'

'It's doing a very good job!'

She laughed and so did George, who started to run over the unsteady bridge, molten lava whizzing harmlessly overhead. The Asebeian gave up trying to cut the rope and bounded towards the forest.

A few seconds later, there was a tremendous crack and a thud. Astrid looked around,

'Oh, that's clever of it – look, George!'

George gasped at the sight of the creature carrying a huge tree in its hands. It had pulled it out of the ground – roots and all.

The children guessed the intentions of the giant and quickened their pace. They cleared the bridge just as the creature tossed the tree across the gorge. With a mighty thud, it spanned the gap. They ran. They didn't wait to see the Asebeian climbing along the tree trunk. It wobbled with the weight of the monster. The Asebeian leapt off the tree an instant before it tumbled into the gorge. It burst into flames before it reached the bottom. Whinger moaned as he watched the tree sizzle in the lava,

'Now we can't get back!'

'Shut up, will yer!' roared Grudge. 'We'll get another tree once we catch the brat.'

'Oh, do stop wasting time!' exclaimed Sneaky. 'The further he gets away, the weaker we'll become, so put some effort into it.'

Astrid had led George on to a hidden path through the forest.

'The Asebeian doesn't know about this path. Only citizens of Melodious know of it.' They were soon at the foot of a rocky hill. Astrid gave George another fire berry and ate one herself.

'We'll both need the strength for the climb. How's your chest?'

'It's a bit sore, but I'm okay. I'll manage the climb. But thanks for asking.'

'Keep still.' She blew more of the crystals she had called *The Tears of Daionas* into George's face. Once more he felt that a refreshing breeze had filled his lungs.
Astrid sensed George's awkwardness.

'You're not used to people being kind to you are you?'

He shook his head.

'I'm not used to kids my own age being nice to me, except Glen my best friend. I've had a few adults who are kind, like my Mum and Mr Johnson.'

'You must just be shy of girls then.' She grinned and he blushed.

'You want to help Glen, don't you?' George nodded in surprise.

'Well, I'm sure you will help him,' she said putting on the rucksack again.

'Let me carry that for you.'

'Oh thanks, but it's lighter now and besides, you need the strength for the climb.'

'What about the Asebeian? Won't it catch up?'

'It might, but not yet – race you to the top!'

The jutting rocks helped the children climb the hill without too much difficulty. Once in a while they slipped and grazed their knees. Astrid had tied a rope to George and led the way. She waited patiently for him. He was weaker than he realised. When they reached the top, George caught sight of himself in a pool of clear water.

'What a mess! My Mum will have a fit when she sees me.'

George's clothes were little more than rags. His shoes were falling apart. Astrid untied the rope as he splashed himself with the water, in a vain effort to clean off the dirt. He managed to spread it evenly across his face. She burst into delighted laughter. George glared at her. She poked out her tongue at him. He splashed some water at her, so she pushed him into the pool. He grabbed hold of her. She lost her balance and splashed down next to him. The water came up to their waists. Both giggled uncontrollably.

Every time one stopped laughing, the other would set them off again. For one glorious, blissful moment, they forgot all their troubles. They laughed and laughed, clutching their sides until they could laugh no more. The Asebeian picked her up and hurled her off the hill onto the jagged rocks below. She didn't even have time to scream.

George ran to the edge of the cliff. There was no sign of Astrid. He was stunned. His mind couldn't take in what had just happened. He turned to look at the Asebeian with its five heads grinning maliciously at him. Neither George nor Astrid had seen the sudden arrival of the creature. George recovered from the shock as anger bubbled up inside him. He picked up stones and threw them at the heads.

'You murderer! Take that!' George's rage was so strong that he advanced on the ogre with no thought for his own safety. All he could think about was Astrid. He wanted to help her – to climb down and find her body. The Asebeian was in his way. He dashed around the creature in an effort to lure it to the edge of the cliff. He ran under the giant's legs. It twisted and turned, failing to grab hold of him. Then George picked up heavier stones when he saw that the Asebeian had its back to the cliff's edge. He hurled the rocks at it.

'Get out of my way! You don't scare me anymore!'

The monster backed away, moving closer to the edge. George kept up his advance, ignoring the pleas of the heads for him to stop. Suddenly it stood still. It let the stones bounce off it. All the heads spoke in chorus,

'Zenobiel… Zenobiel… Zenobiel.'

George thought that the beast was swearing at him. He was greatly mistaken. As the heads chanted the strange word, they grew stronger. The sky darkened. Shadows fell everywhere. The Asebeian pointed to something behind George.

He turned to see the sinister mouth of a cave. For the first time, he took notice of his surroundings – he had been in that cave before. George let go of the stones. They made a dull thud on the ground. A clamp closed around his chest. His stomach flipped over. His legs failed him. He slumped to the ground. The Asebeian knelt down and bowed in worship. It continued to chant,

'Zenobiel, Zenobiel.' The chanting became a whisper, and then the creature fell silent. The heads wore the look of triumph. They gazed reverently towards the cave.

George stared at the cave mouth with mounting horror. He saw the burning red eyes first. They transfixed him. He couldn't run. He couldn't move. He could only watch as his doom approached. The head was shaped like a man's, but it had a lion's mouth with the fangs of a cobra. For the first time, George was able to see the entire monster as it emerged from the cave.

Under the terrifying head protruded pointed fins, just above its powerful arms. A colossal snake's body followed, rising upwards to tower above George like a giraffe. George couldn't believe his ears – there was the sound of scuttling legs. The snake part of the creature was only the neck – the body was a gigantic scorpion, with an armoured tail and deadly sting.

When the nightmare creature moved, it hugged the ground, making it difficult for George to guess its true size. Its bluish-black body was covered in scales and razor-sharp teeth ran along its spine. The living shadow crept towards him. And darkness followed. George's last remaining strength poured out like water from a tap. The darkness overpowered him. He found himself flat on his face.

The Asebeian was bent in worship. Respectfully, it said,

'Zenobiel... My master!'

'Well done, my faithful one.' Zenobiel looked George in the eyes, saying,

'Are you bowing before the King of Shadowsss as well, George?'

He urged his legs to stand. It was a great effort but he managed it.

'No, I am not bowing to you! I will never bow to you!'

The voice of Zenobiel had a hypnotic effect.

'I see that you have acquired courage, George. That can be useful to me.'

'I will not be useful to you!'

'Oh, listen how he speaks to the King,' cried Sneaky, 'George, you must show respect to your master.'

'He's not my master!' George gained confidence with each act of defiance. But he was unprepared when the ruler of shadows said,

'But you are already my ssservant. You have alwaysss ssserved me. Who do you think built Asebeia? Asebeia is my creation, my child. My spirit flowssss through it. I gave it birth.'

George didn't have time to question the strange way Zenobiel described the city. Instead he was beginning to understand something very distasteful about himself.

'That is right, George. Your unwillingness to forgive servessss me ssstill. I will reward you greatly if you return to Asebeia.'

George's mind was clear now. He had enjoyed the delights of the Fun Palace. If Luminous had not sung the song, he would have played with the train set forever. He also knew that his thirst for revenge bound him to this vile creature. He understood that not forgiving his father or the bullies imprisoned his heart.

'Yesss, yesss,' oozed Zenobiel.

'I see your thoughts. You know the truth. You are mine. I can reward you with riches beyond your dreams. I will forgive you your disrespect. I will forgive your futile attempt to escape. Just go back to the city.' Zenobiel paused; he sensed that George wasn't interested in riches.

'If you continue to serve me I will make you strong. Yesss, you will have a powerful body without disease. Imagine George, a body without asthma...'

A body without asthma, thought George; *that would be wonderful.*

'Yess, it would be wonderful. I will turn you into a mighty warrior. You will fight and be strong. I see it clearly. You will be very useful to me. You could bring many into my city. You could bring your family too. They will join your father – that hateful person who took away your train set.'

'NO!' shouted George. 'I will not let you hurt my family and though I find it hard to forgive, I will try. I think Daionas will help me.'

'Do not mention that name!'

'I will mention it. Astrid told me that I could call for Daionas and that's what I'll do.' George raised his voice,

'Daionas! Daionas – whoever you are – please help me!'

Zenobiel howled and struck at George.

The blow knocked him to the ground. The sting lunged towards his head. It stuck in the earth. George crawled away. He was pinned down by Zenobiel's arm.

'You call in vain, boy. He will not answer you.'

'Yes he will!'

'No, he will not. And do you want to know why?'

'I... I... don't care why.'

'There is no such person as Daionas. He does not exist. There is no such place as Melodious either. There is no light, only darkness and despair.'

The memory of the song trickled into his mind. The trickle became a stream; the stream became a flood. George managed to free himself. He dived out of the way of another blow and scrambled to his feet.

'You're lying!' he shouted. 'I've seen Luminous. He set me free from the cell.'

Zenobiel's laugh was chilling.

'No, you did not see him. He wasss a dream.'

'Now I know you're lying – Astrid helped me. She introduced me to Luminous and told me about Daionas.'

'Astrid? Who is Astrid? Astrid is another dream. You broke out of your cell on your own, George.' The eyes hypnotised him, clouding his mind. The song rang in his ears. It blew away the doubt.

'No! Daionas is real! You are the lie! I defy you – I will never serve you again. I will serve King Daionas – if he will let me.'

The beast flared into a rage.

'I hate this king! I hate his servants! And if you will not serve me, then I will feast upon your flesh!'

He grabbed hold of George, pinning him to the ground. The sting was raised up, poised to strike at George's heart. It came down with tremendous force. George had shut his eyes. He expected to be overpowered by pain. It never came. He heard the flapping of wings and a powerful wind blew against his face. He opened his eyes to see Zenobiel lying a few metres away from him, on his back, struggling like a helpless beetle.

A magnificent eagle hovered overhead; it dwarfed the monster. The feathers shone with the brilliance of the sun. The shadows fled; so did the Asebeian, howling in terror. Zenobiel rolled over and sped towards George. Another blow from the eagle sent him flying. Every time Zenobiel moved, the eagle swiped him. Zenobiel wriggled in the dust. The eagle picked George up and placed him in the cave, then blocked the entrance with a large boulder. There was a gap big enough to allow George to see the fierce battle that followed.

Zenobiel repeatedly thrust the sting towards the golden body. The eagle was swift. Zenobiel thrashed at thin air. George's ears were battered by blood-curdling howls but the eagle's powerful wings sounded like the rush of a mighty waterfall. The eagle flipped the monster over, pressing its giant talons against Zenobiel's belly. Zenobiel couldn't get up. He lashed with his tail and the sting buried itself in the eagle. The bird's head darted quicker than the eye could see. There was a mighty snap. Zenobiel's sting was cut clean off the tail. Black blood spattered onto the ground. Zenobiel writhed in agony.

George covered his ears, but he could still hear the hideous screams. The monster grabbed its tail and spat upon it; making the wound hiss. The spittle formed a bubble and the bleeding stopped. The eagle watched, waiting for Zenobiel's next move.

George recoiled in horror when he saw Zenobiel heading for him. The eagle pounced upon Zenobiel's back. The monster's neck whipped around. Its fangs sank deep into the eagle's leg, filling its body with more poison. Screeching, the bird crashed to the ground. It became limp. Its great golden chest heaved up and down, up and down. Then it stopped. All was quiet. Darkness crept back. Zenobiel gloated over his enemy's lifeless body, hitting it to make sure that the eagle was dead. In a strangely calm voice he said,

'Now I am the only King. My shadow will fill the universe. You are a fool – a fool to give your life to save a worthless brat. I will enjoy feasting upon his bones, and then I will devour his family. My servants will attack your pitiful city. I will destroy it.' He dug his claws deep into the bird's neck. 'You have given me everything.'

The monster's head turned slowly. Its evil eyes stared at the cave. George felt that they bored straight through the boulder and into his soul. He fled to the back of the cave, wedging himself in a crevice. He heard the sound of scratching and scraping on the boulder. Zenobiel screamed as he pounded against the rock – he could not move the boulder placed there by his enemy. There was silence – a deathly, weird silence that seemed to last forever. George waited with bated breath. Had the creature gone or was it just teasing him? He leapt as the cave shuddered.

George clasped his hands around his ears; the crunching and cracking was deafening. The dust made him cough and he freed himself from the crevice as the roof of the cave disappeared. Light flooded the cave. George ran to the gap in the boulder. His eyes widened and his jaw dropped. The eagle, glowing brighter than before, flew in a circle above its prey. It held a huge rock – the roof of the cave – in its talons.

George cheered as half a mountain came crashing down on Zenobiel's head. There was a sickening crunch, and then the ground opened up and swallowed the beast. Fire spewed up as the evil one fell screaming into the depths of the earth.

The majestic bird removed the boulder from the mouth of the cave and looked directly at George. Its sparkling eyes were warm and friendly. George stood trembling in awe.

'I... I thought that you were dead – I saw Zenobiel bite your leg... and... you were all floppy – you looked dead.'
The eagle spoke directly into George's mind.

I did allow the darkness to put me out for a moment. But only for a moment, because there is no darkness in me and the darkness can never overpower the Light. Light always chases the darkness away.

'Oh!'

I am Daionas.

'Thought so, but I didn't expect you to be an eagle.'

What did you expect me to be?

'Er...I really don't know; something like the Seraphim I suppose. Oh no! Your leg is bleeding!' Blood trickled from the wound in the bird's heel. When George saw it, he knew exactly what to do.

Chapter Twelve

MELODIOUS

George was flying high above the clouds. The mountains were mere bumps on the landscape far below. It was exhilarating. The air rushed past him. Though his top was bare, he didn't feel the cold. He had removed his shirt and vest after the battle, and with them he had made a crude bandage for the eagle's wounded leg. He buried himself in the eagle's feathers. At first glance they appeared to be made out of pure gold leaf. Closer inspection revealed that the glow came from within Daionas, who radiated light. As he watched the ever-changing landscape below, he was glad that he didn't have to walk.

Another sound joined the beating of the powerful wings. It was music – glorious music, filling the air. It was so beautiful; George could never have imagined it. A spring of joy bubbled in his heart and washed away all his despair. He could hear both Seraphim and humans singing a joyous melody.

Emerging from silver clouds in front of them was the golden city. It was so dazzling that George had to shade his eyes. The city rested on the top of a gigantic mountain. George couldn't wait to get there.

'Faster,' he urged. 'Faster!'
But the eagle never altered his speed.

Then, without warning, the majestic bird dived and landed on the mountain. A wall of strange blue flame towered over George. The flame surrounded the city. There was no way around it and no way under it. George half expected the eagle to command the wall to disappear, but that did not happen. A knot of fear returned to his stomach as it dawned upon him that he must go through the flames.

'I... I... don't think I can walk through that,' he said, with nervous laughter. 'Is there no other way?'

Not if you want to be free from that.

George looked to see the Asebeian heading his way.

'How did that get here?'

You brought it with you – it is part of you.

'Can't you blast it or something?'

In answer, the eagle spread his wings. He shone brighter than the sun. George closed his eyes. There was a noise like a mighty flood. When George opened his eyes, a man stood in front of him. He was a man of awesome power and majesty – a being of warm glowing light. He wore the robes and crown of a king. His face shimmered with joy. His eyes were brilliant, sparkling like diamonds. They were penetrating eyes, yet warm and full of compassion. George couldn't look into them.

At first, George thought that the eagle had flown away, but then he spied teeth marks on the king's heel. They were the punctures from Zenobiel's fangs. George realised that just as the Seraphim had the ability to change shape, so did their king. He bowed in respect. He trembled with a mixture of fear and joy. A mighty hand fell gently upon his head.

'Do not be afraid.' The voice of the king was commanding and compassionate. It was musical, sounding like a million orchestras playing in perfect harmony.

'Stand on your feet, George, and look at me.' George stood up, but avoided the king's eyes.

'Thank you for the bandage. Your act of kindness, when I was weary from battle will not be forgotten.'

George stared at his tatty shoes, not daring to raise his head. Daionas asked gently, 'Why do you not look at me?'

'I'm not good enough to look at you.'

'That is a good answer, but do not worry. I can and will overcome the darkness that is in your heart. Look at the Asebeian.'

The creature was shaking. The heads were full of terror and confusion.

'It has no power over you, unless you give in to it. The longing for revenge creeps into your heart.'

At last George looked into the eyes of Daionas. 'Your Majesty, I *do* want to forgive my Dad.'

'I know you do, George. But there remains the desire to hurt those who bullied you.'

'I know... I know. I think of Helen, Stipe and their gangs and I feel angry. Then I think of the teachers at "Dunghill" school, especially Stenching. He's worse than that thing.' George pointed to the Asebeian without noticing how it was no longer afraid.

'It's just not fair!'

'What is not fair? That they get away with the things they have done, or that you want to destroy them?'

'Both, I suppose.' George shrugged his shoulders.

'But Your Majesty, they should be stopped. If they bully me, they will bully others too.'

The king nodded in agreement,

'That is very true. However, you are the wrong person to deal with them. You would not stop at paying them back for what they did to you. Your craving for revenge made you want to kill them.' The king knelt down in front of George and gently held his shoulders. 'In no time at all you would be consumed by your hatred. Eventually, you would become the very thing you despise. Look at how your anger and hatred are feeding the Asebeian'

George was shocked to see that the giant was twice its original size, and the heads were uglier and fiercer than before.

'I am preventing this monster from doing any further harm. Do you not realise George; this is what you are like on the inside? If you continue to thirst for revenge, you will be its slave forever. Only the power of forgiveness can defeat it.'

George sighed deeply, 'But if I do forgive all the bullies, won't I be letting them get away with it?'

Daionas smiled, 'No, you will not. You must let the authorities deal with them, for that is their purpose. Because they are not personally involved, they can see that justice is done.'

'But what if the authorities do nothing? The head at "Dunghill" was useless at dealing with the bullies.'

'Then, my friend, you must trust a higher authority. Will you trust me, George? Will you believe me, when I say that I will sort out Dunhill School?'

'Yes I will! I really hate this creature and I want to be free of it. But... um... I don't seem to be able to forgive.'

'Then let me help you. Take my hand, and turn your back on all the wrong emotions that control you.'

George obeyed and turned his back on the Asebeian. The king walked towards the wall of fire, taking George with him. 'At this moment in time, you have no strength of your own to forgive, though that is what you want to do. Once you have gone through this wall, you will be able to do the impossible.'

George's hand trembled in the king's. Together they passed through the flames. There was a rushing noise in his ears. His body shook. He felt pins and needles bursting all over his skin. The fire was warm like a hot bath. As he breathed in, the flames shot straight to his heart. The flame burned inside him and consumed all his hatred. He no longer felt fearful and insecure. Now he was strong and full of confidence.

He looked behind him to the Asebeian. It was struggling against the compulsion to follow. It lost its fight and stepped into the flames. George didn't watch it writhe in agony.

He returned his gaze to the city ahead, greatly relieved to be free from the loathsome creature. Once through the wall of fire, he was astonished to discover that he was completely clean and dressed in the clothes of a prince. He was wearing a white shirt and trousers. Over these he wore a blue robe, which was richly embroidered and tied with a golden sash. On his head was a little golden crown.

There were more wonders. Standing before George, were five boys clothed in white. Their faces were familiar. They had once been Spook, Bile, Whinger, Sneaky and Grudge.

'Hello, George,' they said as they faded from view.

George looked up at Daionas and frowned,

'What happened to the Asebeian?'

'It has been transformed into your invisible friends, who will help you when you need strength.'

'I don't get it.'

The King laughed.

'You still need fear, though this is a different kind of fear. It is the fear of danger. Without this fear you would put your hand in a normal fire, or stand too close to the edge of a cliff. It is also the respect for what is right and good. This fear will prevent you from doing evil things because you will be afraid to offend me.'

'I understand now, but what about anger? I thought that was wrong too.'

'Just as there is a right kind of fear, so there is a right kind of anger. This anger will never let you lose control. It will give you the strength to fight evil, just as you did when you threw rocks at the Asebeian and defied Zenobiel.'

They were approaching the gates of the city. Daionas continued explaining. 'Whinger has changed to compassion. He will help you feel pity for those in need and prompt you to help them. Sneaky is now honesty – you cannot live in the light and be deceitful. Grudge has become goodness. Goodness helps us to hate what is wrong and fight injustice.

These are your inner strengths, George. Use them well and have fun discovering the other gifts I have given you.'

'My head hurts – this is heavy stuff!'

Daionas smiled broadly and said,

'You will be happy to know then, that I have finished telling you 'the heavy stuff.' Let me introduce you to the citizens of Melodious.'

The gates opened to a blast of trumpets, accompanied by cheers of praise and greetings. George was overwhelmed by the welcome and by the sights and sounds of the city. Overhead flew the creatures of fire called the Seraphim. Seeing so many made him tingle with electricity. For the first time, George could understand the words of the song they sang. No language on earth could do them justice. His heart leapt with a joy so great he couldn't put it into words. He stood listening, as still as a statue, losing all track of time. He wished that his legs could grow roots so that he could stand there forever and never cease listening to the song.

Daionas spoke,

'Their sound is heard throughout my city. As long as you live and breathe, you will hear their melody. The Song will live in your heart from now on. It will accompany you throughout your life, and when the time arises, you will sing the Song to others in the same way Astrid sang the Song to you.'

George looked at the King in alarm. He had forgotten about Astrid.

'What happened to her? Is she all right?'

'Why not ask her yourself?'

George looked in the direction the king pointed. Astrid was bounding towards him. She wore a long, white robe and a little crown on her head. Her infectious laughter reached George before she did. She gave him a friendly hug and held him tight. George was so glad to see her that he wasn't embarrassed by her affection.

'Astrid! You're alive!'

'Well, duh! I'm here aren't I?'

'But I saw the Asebeian hurl you off the cliff. No one could have survived that fall.'

'What you didn't see was Luminous catching me.'

'So he did watch over you after all.'

'Of course he did!' She turned to the king. 'Daionas, can I show George around the city?'

'Certainly. I will see you in a few days, George.'

'Why a few days?'

Astrid pulled on George's arm,

'It will take a few days to see everything. In fact, it'll take a lifetime. There are still things I've yet to see. You'll never get bored here, George.' She produced a little map. It showed that the city and its walls were in the shape of a treble clef. She pointed to a building marked 'Dining Hall.'

'We're going there first. You need to build your strength up and put some flesh on those tired bones.'

The hall was full of tables laden with mouth-watering food from all over the world. It looked gorgeous, but it tasted even better. Each mouthful was a feast of delight. The food was so nourishing that, within a day, George was strong and healthy. His face was no longer sunken, but full of life and joy.

George had never dreamt of being so happy. He felt as though bubbles of happiness were bouncing around inside him. He and Astrid walked for days beside crystal clear rivers, barefoot. No one in Melodious wore anything on their feet. The lush green pastures were warm and safe. There was no danger from sharp stones or metal objects. The children could run freely and splash about in the pure water. They swam under the waterfall, ran through the trees and marvelled at all the animals.

George was amazed to see lions rubbing noses with sheep, horses racing with cheetahs and cats playing happily with dogs. He spent a whole day rubbing the ears and belly of a tiger, and was thrilled when the tiger gave him a ride on its back in return. The tiger took him to a field full of horses and children.

They appeared to be preparing for a race.

'Do you want to join the race, George?' asked Astrid.

'Can I? I mean… will I be able to?'

'Of course you can! Your asthma won't bother you here.' She took off her robe and crown,

'Come on, you can't race dressed like that.' George removed his robe and crown, and then followed Astrid to the starting post.

'Er… Astrid?' he asked, trying to mount a horse. 'How do I get on?'

She giggled, 'You're not going to ride the horse – you're going to race against it.'

'I don't understand.'

'The aim of the race is to beat the horse to the finishing post.' She pointed to two trees in the distance. George looked up at the magnificent black stallion standing beside him.

'There's no way I can beat this horse.'

'Oh, you mustn't beat them, that's cruel.'

George shook his head, but couldn't help grinning.

'What's his name?'

'Your horse is called Spur and mine is called Golden Mane.'

George copied Astrid, lining up with the starting post. There were seven children and seven horses, all were waiting for the starting signal.

Someone blew a trumpet and they were off – speeding down the track. George's heart pumped faster, his chest full of air, his legs like powerful engines pushing him further and faster. The horse whinnied with delight.

Astrid was ahead of them, keeping pace with her white mare. George felt the wind rush through his hair. Spur was in front, but only by centimetres. George concentrated all his energy on rushing forward. He focused on the white tape tied between the two trees. He and Spur overtook Astrid. There were loud cheers from both the Seraphim and the other racers as George burst through the tape at exactly the same moment as Spur.

Astrid ran to him, patted his sweating back and said,

'George, that was brilliant! It was a draw and no-one has ever done that before.'

George gasped, 'I'm not in pain – I feel great!'

'Come on, George. I've got to take you to the Great Hall now.'

'What's in there, Astrid?' he asked, patting Spur on the back,

'Thanks Spur, see you again.' The horse nodded his head in reply.

'What's in the Great Hall, Astrid?' he repeated.

She grinned, 'A big surprise.'

Chapter Thirteen

A CITIZEN OF MELODIOUS

The Great Hall was crammed with so many people, the number was impossible to estimate. It wasn't the fact that the hall was full of people from all over the world, representing all the peoples of the Earth that astounded him. It was the fact that they all appeared to be children. When he spoke to them, he realised that they were much older and wiser than they looked. Astrid helped George onto a raised platform, where he stood next to the king. All became quiet and still. Something very important and solemn was about to take place.

Daionas placed his hand upon George; his face was lit with a smile.

'My children. My friends. It is with indescribable joy that I present to you this day a new citizen of Melodious.' The hall filled with cheers and applause. Daionas raised his hand for quiet.

'Today, I welcome George William Tweedie as a citizen of this golden city.'

George had been completely unprepared for this welcome and gazed in silent wonder as Daionas put a ring on his finger. As he handed George a golden certificate, he said, 'Once you have been made a citizen of Melodious, you will always be a citizen. That will never change, even when you are in a far off land. Nothing and no-one can take this away from you.'

He shook George's right hand and the whole city burst into praise.

'Astrid, may I borrow George?' The king's eyes twinkled. Astrid laughed and bounced off to talk with someone else.

Daionas introduced George to many of his fellow citizens and then he took George for a walk under the massive trees in one of the parks. The leaves rustled in the gentle breeze and bird song descended from the tops. Through the trees George could see Astrid, sitting on a hill. She was looking wistfully at a door in the east wall. He was about to run to her when Daionas held him back.

'Let her be on her own for a while.'

'What is she looking at?'

'At that door; behind it is something very precious to her and she longs to go through.'

'Why doesn't she, then?'

'Because those who go through that door never return.'

George was alarmed, but the King smiled. 'Do not be afraid of that door, George, because there is only goodness behind it. On this side of that wall, the citizens of Melodious can come and go as they please. Once they go through that door, they enter my never-ending kingdom and live in Melodious forever.'

'Can I live in Melodious forever, Your Majesty?'

'One day you will, when I decide; but, for now, you will live in two worlds. But never forget, you will always be a citizen of Melodious.'

'Has no one ever come back through that door?'

'I am the only one.'

They continued their walk in silence for quite some time. Then at last George asked the question that had been on his mind ever since his adventure had begun. 'What is this place – this strange dream I'm in?'

'It is called Rûah – the invisible world.'

'It looks visible to me, Your Majesty.'

'That is because you are in this world at the moment so, naturally, you can see it.'

'Rûah is a strange word. What does it mean, Your Majesty?'

'It is a word with many meanings – wind, breath, spirit. You are in a spiritual world. This world is a reflection of the world that can be seen. What is unseen in your world is made visible here.'

'Oh.' George shook his head. 'I don't really understand what you are saying, Your Majesty.'

'You do not have to understand everything in order to enjoy it; neither do you need to address me as 'Your Majesty.' You may call me Daionas, for though you are not my equal, you are my friend.'

George went quiet. He wasn't used to calling adults by their first names, especially a person with so much authority. He didn't want to be too familiar, in case he showed disrespect.

'Do not worry, George. You will never disrespect me. And you will get used to many things here. Think of Melodious as your home. This is where you belong. This is where your dreams will bring you. I have made your dreams a doorway into this world. It is really the Song that brought you here.' His eyes became distant and wistful.

'There was a time when everyone could understand my Song and delighted in its melody. Then Zenobiel, one of my Seraphim, rebelled against me. He wanted power... he sought total power. His aim was to control the lives of others and to enslave them to his will. He hates my Song because it sets the heart free. When he deserted me, he became twisted into the fiend you saw and built the city of rebellion. He deafens ears to music because he wants to imprison the heart with sadness.'

He stopped and turned to look at George. 'I would have everyone hear my song, but there are some who simply do not wish to hear. They would rather listen to the lies of my enemy.'

'Why is music important?' asked George, 'I mean, people seem to need music.'

'Someone in your world once called music, "The harmonious voice of creation, an echo of the invisible world."'

'You mean an echo of this world?'

'That is correct. Good music echoes the Song the Seraphim sing. Bad music is like the noise in Asebeia.'

'But people like different kinds of music, so what do you mean by "good" and "bad"?'

'Good music, whatever the style, creates positive feelings and attitudes. It can soothe a troubled mind and create feelings of peace within. Bad music does the exact opposite. It can over excite a person; even make them aggressive or spiteful.'

He looked at George, who suddenly remembered how he had wanted to hurt others when he was singing *I hate Mondays*. Daionas nodded and added,

'Music is a powerful tool in communicating ideas.'

'I think I understand, though not everything.'

'One day you will understand all that you need to.' Daionas became grave.

'Meanwhile, there is something I want you to do for me. It is difficult and very dangerous.'

'Just ask and I will do anything for you.'
The smile on the king's face made it even brighter.

'Well done, George! You are willing to serve me, though you do not know what the task is.'

'What do you want me to do?'

'You are to rescue three people from Asebeia. Once you have reached the wooden bridge, my Seraphim will bring them here to Melodious. Then you will return home.' George was saddened at the thought of returning home, although he did miss his family.

'Who do you want me to rescue?'

'One is a friend, one an enemy and the other... is your own father.'

'My Dad's in Asebeia?'

'Yes, he is, and we must get to him before he fades away altogether. Do you remember the old man you sang the Song to? It was not a mistake to call him "Pops".'

'That old man is my Dad?' George stared at Daionas in amazement.

'He is indeed. That's why you were drawn to him.'

'Did he really kill someone?'

'Come, let us sit down under that tree by the river and I will tell you a story about a very brave man.' They sat on the soft, thick grass by a willow. The river was flowing gently and the restful surroundings were in stark contrast to the story Daionas related to George.

'As you know, your father was in the Middle East during one of the many savage conflicts that arise in those troubled lands. He was serving dinner in the Mess tent, when a terrorist entered, firing a machine gun. There were two hundred men and women in the tent at the time. Five were killed instantly and three were wounded, but your father prevented more deaths.

When everyone else dived for cover, your father ran towards the gunman and hit him with a heavy saucepan. Your father was injured but struggled with the terrorist, who drew out a knife. In the fight, your father unintentionally stabbed the terrorist and killed him.

The whole episode took only minutes. If your father had not acted as he did, more people would have died that day. The tent had been full of British and American troops at the time, so he was awarded those countries' highest honours. Your father spent a long time in hospital before returning home.'

'I didn't know any of this,' said George thoughtfully. 'I didn't realise that my Dad was a hero.'

'Your father did not want anyone to know. He threw away his medals. They would have been lost, if your mother had not retrieved them.'

'Why did he throw them away?'

Daionas placed his hand gently on George's shoulder. There were tears in his eyes as he said,

'Because your father was affected by a deeper wound than that made by a knife or a bullet; he believed he was responsible for the man's death. He had never been in action before and was troubled by the many terrible things he saw. Your father is a chef, not a warrior; he had never taken another life. He blamed himself for failing to prevent those deaths that day. Then Zenobiel suffocated him with guilt and despair. Though I cannot excuse all his behaviour since he returned home, I do understand the pain he is in. Your father is wasting away. He needs to be set free, to come here and be young again. You are the one to help him.'

George sprang to his feet and shouted with eagerness,

'I'll go now!'

Daionas got up too and together they headed for a group of children and Seraphim talking by another stream.

'George, you must understand that Zenobiel will not let your father go without a fight.'

'I thought Zenobiel was dead. I saw you smash his head in with a rock.'

'Zenobiel is merely wounded; even so, I have robbed him of most of his power, but he deceives himself. He believes that he has the same power he once possessed, so he will try to stop you. He will fail, because I have given you my power to defeat him.'

'Me? But Daionas, I'm only a kid. I'm a weakling – I don't know how to fight that thing.'

'You did not listen; I have given you *my* power to defeat the enemy. When you meet Zenobiel again, you will wield my sword. Listen carefully; I have other things to tell you that you need to know.' Talking together, they reached the small group of Melodians, which included Astrid, Luminous and some other Seraphim. George was introduced to one named Nova. He stared in wonder at the beautiful creature.

'I didn't know there was girl Seraphim.'

Nova looked at George with sparkling eyes, and said,

'I am not a girl. I am a Seraphim.'

George couldn't take his eyes off Nova, not until Astrid went up to him and nudged him.

'Are you ready, George?' she asked.

'Are you coming too?'

'Of course I am! You didn't think I'd leave all the fun to you, did you?'

Daionas gave a wonderful, gentle, laugh, saying,

'Astrid's enthusiasm will eventually rub off on you, George. Prepare for your adventure without delay.'

Before setting out, the children changed into sensible clothes for their adventure: jeans, sweatshirt, a jacket and tough boots. Both carried a rucksack with a flask of milk, loaves of bread and several fire berries. George had marvelled at the trees that produced the unusual fruit. They were called Lumin trees. They were so tall that only the Seraphim could pick the berries.

The leaves were coloured yellow, green and different shades of red, not from the dying breaths of autumn, but from the fire emitted by the Seraphim flying above the treetops. The fire of the Seraphim became liquid like raindrops and rested upon the branches. This liquid light empowered the fruit with life and the ability to heal. These trees were the oldest things in Melodious, having been planted by Daionas himself, before a single golden brick had been laid.

When they were ready, George flew with Luminous while Astrid flew with Nova. His mind was racing ahead. He didn't know whether to be excited or afraid. He decided to be both.

Chapter Fourteen

BACK TO ASEBEIA

The children reached the city at midnight, when the Asebeians were in a deep sleep. The two Seraphim changed into human form. Nova had red hair and startling brown eyes.

'Stop gawping at Nova!' hissed Astrid. George's cheeks went pink. Astrid led them to a deserted part of the city. She stood above a manhole cover embedded in the concrete.

'We're not going down a sewer, are we?' asked George in disgust.

'Yeah – it's called the pit. It's where the Asebeians dump those who are no longer useful to them. The people down here are too weak to work anymore.'

George helped Astrid remove the manhole cover. Shyly, he said to Nova and Luminous, 'Er... um... you wait here and guard us – that's an order from the King! And if the Asebeians chase us, you are to paralyse them.'

'Understood,' they replied, bowing to George.
Astrid grinned, 'Don't worry, George, you'll soon get the hang of leading.'

'But they're Seraphim!'

'And our servants, too.'

'Wow!' he whispered.

He lowered Astrid down the manhole first, and then he joined her. The stench made their heads swim. They blew *Tears of Daionas* into each other's faces; the crystals melted on contact and masked the smell. The pit filled with light from the lanterns they carried.

'Ugh!' blurted Astrid.

'What's up?'

'I've just stood in something unmentionable.'

'Well, don't mention it then.'

'Very funny.' She shook her foot in an attempt to rid it of the muck.

George was impatient,

'Don't waste time. Let's find them before they are beyond our help.' But instead of rushing off, he stood still, thinking about his sister.

'Your sister isn't down here, George, she's not the friend Daionas mentioned. But don't give up hope.'

'How did you know what I was thinking?'

'You forget,' she grinned mischievously. 'I know a lot about you.'

'I'll never get used to this mind-reading stuff!'

'You will. Now come on, and stop wasting time!' They both giggled.

They followed the long tunnel, stooping lower the further they went. There were rows of people chained to the damp walls.

'It's a pity that we can't save them all,' sighed George.

'Don't worry. Just as Daionas sent me for you and you for your father, he'll send others down here – he tends to send for people one at a time.'

'But why?' snapped George, 'He could send an army against this place and rescue the lot!'

'I don't know – and there's no need to get stroppy.'

'Sorry, Astrid.' George tripped over something sticking out of the ground – it was a boy's head. He was buried in muck up to his neck. George knelt down and exclaimed,

'Glen! I never thought it would be you.'

'Get away! Get away!'

126

George was startled. 'Why is he frightened of me, Astrid?'

'He thinks you're his Asebeian. Sing The Song.'

The song was always in his mind and, as he sang it to Glen, the light grew in strength. It shimmered in the air and formed the shape of two glittering swords. Astrid and George took the swords and pushed them into the ground. Immediately, a light surrounded Glen and he floated out of the sludge. They wiped his face and gave him some milk. His strength slowly returned as he ate some bread.

It was while they were waiting that George saw him. He was chained to the wall, a few feet away from Glen.

'Mr Stenching! So you're the enemy I must rescue.' George moved in front of Mr Stenching. His pale face no longer resembled a kindly grandfather figure. His cruel nature was revealed in all its repulsiveness. Thin, weak and dying though he was, his eyes held George with a hate-filled stare.

'Tweedie! What are you doing with that knife? I knew you were trouble, the moment I saw you. Come to kill me, eh?'

George sighed,

'I don't hate you now and I'm sorry I imagined blowing you to bits.' George smashed the sword against the chains. Nothing happened.

'Missed me! I'll have you, Tweedledum. Mark my words.' George ignored the insults. He sang the song and tried again to break the chains, but once again the sword didn't make a dent.

'Stop this at once, boy! And stop making that terrible noise.'

'I don't understand this.' George shook his head. 'I was supposed to come for an enemy.'

'So that's it!' spat the teacher. 'Come to get me, have you? You'll regret this. You'll end up in prison, you will. Your sort always does.'

'Oh do be quiet! I'm trying to free you. Don't you know where you are?'

'What are you rambling on about, boy? Your wooden head is burning up. That's it – he's mad. Mad, you are – we're in the classroom. Get back to work this instant. I'll put you back in the gym, I will. Make you work until you drop. I'll get you, Tweedledum.'

'It's Tweedie, you brute!' shouted Astrid. 'And it's you who will end up in prison.'

'What? A girl! What are you doing here? Girls are not allowed in Dunhill.'

Astrid pulled George away.

'You can't help him, George.'

'But I thought I had to help an enemy?'

'Wrong enemy. He's beyond anyone's help. He's been cruel to children like you for years. We have no choice but to leave him. Cheer up, your friend is stronger now.'

George returned to Glen, who finally recognised him.

'George?'

'Yes, it's me.'

'Excellent! But you shouldn't have pulled me out. I was being punished for what I did to my Mum and Dad. I deserve to be here for causing their divorce.'

'You didn't cause it. They still love you, but you can't get them back together. They decided not to be married anymore – that's not your fault.'

Glen smiled.

'You're a good friend, George.'

'Don't mention it. I've been told by the King of Light to tell you that good will come out of this – whatever that means. You mustn't listen to the lies of the Asebeian anymore.'

'What's an As...are...bean?'

'It's that monster that's been bothering you but it's being sorted out by some friends of ours.' He handed Glen a fire berry. 'Eat this. It'll give you strength. I'll be back in a minute.'

'Come with me,' said Astrid, pulling on George's arm, 'I think I've found the enemy. I'll take her and Glen with me to the bridge, while you get your dad.'

'But I don't know where he is.'

She pointed to a tiny opening in the bricks.

'He's in there.'

George headed for the hole but Astrid pulled him back,

'First, rescue the enemy.'

'Of course, it's just… '

'You don't have to explain.'

George found himself in a side cell. He gasped – it was unlike anything else in that dirty place. He was looking into the room of a very rich girl. The walls were covered in expensive wallpaper and fine paintings. Every bit of furniture, including the bed, would not have looked out of place in the room of a princess. On a desk was a state-of-the-art computer, a television set and Hi-Fi system. However, the last item wasn't playing music. The only sound coming out of the speakers was the irritating high-pitched whistle that was always present in Asebeia.

In a lonely corner of the room there was something that took George's breath away. At first sight, it appeared to be a skeleton buried beneath a pile of fashionable clothes and jewellery. Then he realised that the bones had a thin covering of flesh on them. Her once-thick, blond hair was falling out and her blue eyes had sunk into her face. They stared blankly, revealing the emptiness within.

Astrid shuddered.

'Who is she?'

'It's Helen Risdale,' replied George in a whisper. 'She was the ringleader of the bullies in one of my junior schools. All she cared about was her image and material things.'

'Look at her clothes – they have chunks torn out of them, as if she's been trying to eat them.'

'Let's get her out of here.'

He wiped a tear from his eyes and strode towards Helen. He raised the sword. It cut straight through the golden chain that hung from the roof of the cell and was fastened around her. She fell further into the pile of clothes.

George and Astrid picked her up and carried her out of the cell, placing her gently beside Glen. She looked as though she were dead – she was so still. He blew *Tears of Daionas* into her face. It came alive and her eyes sparkled. She stared at George with a puzzled look.

'George? George Tweedie? Is it really you?'

'Yeah. It's me all right.'

'What are you doing here?'

'Believe it or not, I've come to rescue you.'

'Rescue me? From that creature with many heads?'

'That's right – and from this expensive prison of yours.'

'But why? After all that I did to you, you're helping me? What's the catch?'

'There isn't one. Drink this milk, Helen, and eat this. You must get your strength back. There'll be plenty of time for questions later.' He gave her a fire berry and while she slowly ate the healing fruit, Astrid pulled George aside, whispering to him.

'George, do you forgive Helen? She was really nasty to you.'

The deep sigh echoed in the tunnel.

'Of course I do! After I went through the wall of fire, my hatred for all the bullies vanished. I don't want to get my own back on them anymore.'

'Sorry, George, I didn't mean to upset you. It's just that you might have felt differently when yer were face to face with your enemy.'

'I do feel different. I feel sorry for her and I don't think she's the enemy at all.'

Helen was able to sit up on her own after eating two fire berries and a small loaf of bread.

'That's Glen!' she exclaimed in surprise. Glen waved feebly at Helen and she asked, 'Who's your friend, George?'

'Oh, I'm sorry. This is Astrid. She'll take you and Glen to Nova. Nova's your Guardian – a bit like a guardian angel.'

'Who's mind-reading now?' said Astrid.

'Oh, I wasn't mind-reading; just worked it out, that's all. Why else would Daionas send two Seraphim?' Astrid replied by blowing a playful raspberry.

'Same to you.' He was about to leave to find his father, when Helen grabbed his heel.

'Sorry for being such a snob and for picking on you.'

'Forget it – I have.'

'Thanks, George, I...'

'Sorry, Helen, I'd love to stay and chat, but I've one more person to help.'

'But I must tell you why I picked on you.'

George looked at her with renewed interest. She took a deep breath and said, 'I was jealous of you.'

He was astonished. 'Jealous? You were jealous of me? But why? Your family is rich and gives you everything.'

'Not everything.' She shook her head. 'I've got plenty of things, but I'm not close to my parents like you are to yours. My mother only takes notice of me if I win prizes or get top marks. My father is never around. I haven't any true friends. Those that hang about me only want me for what they can get out of me. But you have got real friends, like Glen and Astrid.'

George didn't know what to say. He was so surprised by this news. In the end he shook her hand gently, nodded and headed for his father's cell. He paused,

'Thanks for telling me that, Helen. Astrid, can I borrow your rucksack?'

'Of course you can. Your dad will need a lot of food, just to give him enough strength to sit.'

'That bad is he?'

'Sadly, yes.'

Helen and Glen said together,

'Thanks George.'

'Don't mention it,' he replied as he turned to leave. Astrid made ready to take Glen and Helen to safety. Before leaving the tunnel, she shouted after George,

'Bye, George. I'll see you in a few weeks time.'

George was too far away to hear her, having reached the darkest, dirtiest and most revolting part of the pit. Even the light from the lantern was gobbled up by the thick darkness. The foul smell made George feel sick. There was a wall at the end of the tunnel. He stepped towards it and the ground disappeared. He plummeted down a deep hole.

Chapter Fifteen

DAD IN THE PIT

Filthy water gurgled in George's ears. He told himself, *Stop panicking you idiot*! *Find the bottom of the pool and push*! His body shot up. He spluttered and spat foul sewage out of his mouth.

'Ugh! Poo!' He found himself standing in stinking water up to his chest. Frantically, George wiped the filth from his mouth.

'Disgusting! Where's a fire berry?'

It was pitch black and that made it difficult to find the fruit in the rucksack but once he had bitten into the fruit, his mouth was clean and so he sang the song.

Light cut through the dark, as the sword of Daionas reappeared. George grasped the double-edged sword firmly in his right hand. With the sword glowing ever brighter, George could see that he was in a large cavern at the foot of a huge cliff. The climb to the top was impossible.

Chained to the wall of the cave was his father. George's heart ached with the pain of seeing a shadow of the man he called Dad. Fear gripped George as he wondered how he was going to get his father out of the pit.

George, do not be afraid. I am with you.

George spun round, 'Who said that?'

It is I, Daionas, speaking into your mind – listen to my
voice and when in doubt, simply think of me. I will tell you
all that you need to know in order to help your father
escape from this place.

'So that's how Astrid knew all about me! Daionas was
telling her!'

George plunged the sword into the water. Immediately,
the water stopped rising and drained away. Once the water
had gone, George could cut his father loose without the
danger of drowning him.

It took a long time to revive his father. He used up all
the crystals from both rucksacks before there was any sign
of life. He gently lifted the old man's frail head and put the
flask to his lips, helping him to drink the refreshing milk.
The old man opened his eyes. A mist of recognition passed
over his face. He nodded feebly, trying to speak.

'Don't try to speak yet,' said George. He held the flask
until his father had emptied it. With the sword, he cut a
fire berry and placed small pieces straight into his father's
mouth. Once the berries had gone, George put the bread
into the man's trembling hands. He was now able to feed
himself.

George spoke out loud, more to himself than his father,

'I'm just going to stick this sword into the cave wall –
it'll give us light – I lost the lantern when I fell.'

The man sat up, leaning against the wall where he had
been chained. He had been there ever since his encounter
with George in the domed building. The Asebeian in
control of George's father had been terrified that its
prisoner would escape its greedy clutches. So, to prevent
the song from doing any good, it had banished the old man
to the pit.

After an hour of feeding and tender care, the old man
became aware of the boy who sat crossed-legged in front
of him. He looked familiar.

'Thank you.' His voice was hoarse from lack of use.
'Who are you?'

Do not tell him that you are his son George; he needs to

take time to grasp the truth.

'I'm the boy you met in the fun palace; the one who sang *The Song* to you.'

'I remember now. I liked that sound. Will you sing again?'

'Yes, if you like. I know the proper words now, though you won't be able to understand them yet – just let the music wash over you.'

George sang the song of the Seraphim three times, because he could see the wonderful effect it had on his father. With each verse, the old man's eyes grew more alert. Strength, from both food and music, was seeping back into his body. When George ended the song, his father's face looked younger, although it was still horribly thin. He asked George,

'What's your name?'

'George – and your name is William.'

'Is it...? Yes... I remember now – but how did you know that?'

'A friend told me.'

'George? That sounds familiar, somehow. Have we met before?'

'Yes, I told you, in the domed hall.'

'No, that's not what I meant; you look like someone I know very well, like an old friend. No... no,' he shook his head, 'It's... it's more than that. More than a friend... no, sorry – I can't remember.'

'Give it time, Da – I mean William. You'll remember soon enough.'

George, now is the time to confront him.

George took a deep breath.

'William, I've got to tell you what the ogre who put you here is.'

'A foul, filthy beast!'

'Well, yes, but apart from that, it's called an Asebeian. It's all your wrong feelings and actions made alive. It's what we're like inside, when we let hate or fear control us. All your despair is eating away at you, but when you're in

Melodious, you'll be young, because your inside will be right and full of good emotions. Sorry, I wandered off then, trying to work everything out for myself. Anyway, the five heads of the creature represent something in you.'

'Four.'

'Pardon?'

'Four heads – you said it had five. It's only got four ugly heads.' He became afraid, so George held the bony hand in his. A tiny smile crossed his father's worn-out face.

'I forgot,' said George, 'each Asebeian is different.' George wasn't sure how to proceed but Daionas said,

Ask him what names the creature gave to its heads.

'Tell me the names of the heads, one by one, and I'll tell you what they are.'

'I don't understand.'

'One of the heads, on the ogre that captured me, was called Grudge. He was my hatred of others and my craving to get my own back.' George paused. He felt awkward as he remembered how he had hated his father.

'Now I understand, George. One of the heads is nicknamed Stormy by the others.'

'That's easy – he's your bad temper.'

'Well, I don't want it anymore. I'm too tired to be angry and I'm sorry for causing pain to those I love.'

'Good. We're getting there. What's the name of the next head?'

'Void – now let me think, young man.' He shook his head in frustration, 'No, I can't work that one out, but I know that a void is an empty place.'

'Well, that's the emptiness you feel inside. It's also your useless attempts at happiness, like buying swords, china and beer.' George waited as his father nodded in agreement, then he continued, 'None of those things can give you real or lasting happiness. I should know – I treated a train set as if it was a friend, but it only made me happy for a short time. Now I'm happy, knowing that good people care for me.'

'A train set?' said his father, moving closer to him. 'Now why does that sound familiar?'

George ignored the question. 'What does the head called Bale, stand for?'

'How did you know that one of the heads was called Bale?'

'Daionas told me. He is the King of Light, and I'm going to take you to Him.'

His father was lost in thought, so he didn't hear. Finally he said, 'Bale is despair. I've seen many horrible things in a war. Then I've behaved badly towards my family and...'He paused, and then became excited, shouting: 'FAMILY!'

George jumped as his father gripped his hands. His face was alive with recognition,

'That's it – you're my son, aren't you?'

Tears dribbled down George's cheeks,

'Yes, Dad. I am your son, George.' They embraced.

'George, I am so sorry – sorry for everything. I've been a terrible father. You're better off without me.'

'That's not true, Dad.'

Tell him that you love him, George.

That's soppy! George replied, without opening his mouth.

If you will not tell him that you love him, tell him that you are his friend. When you are more mature, you will be able to declare the love a son should have for a father.

'Dad, I forgive you for everything and all your children love you. So does Mum. She loves you very much.'

Pain returned to his father's face.

'George, you mustn't. I neglected my family. I've done terrible things – evil things – I murdered a man.'

'No you didn't, Dad. You're listening to the last and most powerful head of your Asebeian. Tell me its name.'

'I can't remember,' he lied.

'Yes you can!'

'Fit-up! It's called Fit-up – it's always reminding me of my guilt.'

George sighed before saying, 'It's false guilt you feel. Fit-up accuses you of many false things. Things that never happened in the way you remember them.'

'No George! I am guilty. I feel the guilt. You must leave me. Leave me now – I deserve to die!'

He pushed George away, sinking deeper into despair. He looked like a man drowning in his own sadness.

George stood up and raised the sword in the air.

'I know that you're here.' He spoke to the darkness. His voice was steady and full of confidence. 'You're down here with us, aren't you? I can smell your foul stench.'

'Who are you talking to, George?'

'The Asebeian; it's been here all the time. It's heard everything we've said and now it is pouring lies into your mind. *You* don't want me to leave, *it* does. It knows that I carry the means of its doom.' The sword became a beacon in George's hand, banishing the shadows. Hiding in a crevice was the ogre.

As it emerged, rock split and the cave shook violently. In fury it smashed against the cave wall and screamed.

'You don't frighten me you big bully!' yelled George, Are you angry because you've been discovered? Come on then, show your ugly mugs.'

'George!' cried his father, cowering against the wall, you're provoking it!'

'That's the idea Dad!'

The Asebeian towered over them – it was bigger, stronger and uglier than the creature that had imprisoned George. Eight penetrating eyes stared at George. Its revolting faces were twisted in rage and all four heads howled together,

'Leave him alone! He's mine. Get away, boy, or I will crack you in half. I'll tear off your flesh and eat it. Then I'll grind your bones into dust.'

George raised the sword with both hands. He was ready.

'Run away, George!' screamed his father. 'Do as it says, son, – save yourself!'

138

'No. I won't run away. I hold the sword of Daionas. He has given me the right to lop off your heads. It's you who'll taste death!'

The beast's roar was deafening. George stood in front of his father. Razor sharp teeth dripped with spit as the creature roared again. It took slow, careful steps. Closer and closer it came, raising its hands to reveal huge tiger-like claws. Lazily, with its left hand it scratched the wall of the cave – the screeching claws set George's teeth on edge but he held his ground, tensing all his muscles. He never took his eyes off the beast.

'Hurry up, will you! My Dad needs to get home.'

Thud, thud, thud, went the feet of the giant. It bounded towards George. The sword flashed. The creature screamed. Its legs were cut clean in two. Another flash and it lost its legs entirely. George's movements were so quick the monster had no time to think. He wielded the sword again. The right arm was sliced clean off. Another swish filled the air. The left arm plopped onto the ground. The heads were whining, pleading for mercy. It never came. One by one, George lopped off each hideous head. Once the Asebeian lay in pieces at George's feet, the sword vanished.

George sank to the ground in exhaustion. He was amazed by what he had done. His father shot to his feet and picked up his son, holding him tightly. George's father didn't look like an old man anymore. He was himself again. He was still weak and terribly thin, but even so, he was free at last.

George knew from his own experience not to trust appearances – the power of Zenobiel might recreate the Asebeian. It was vital that they left the city. George called for Luminous, who appeared at his command. Very soon, both George and his father stood safely on the far side of the wooden bridge. Daionas appeared in eagle-form to take George's father to Melodious.

After Daionas and his father had left, George was ready to return home, to wake up from his dream. He had the feeling that his life would never be the same again. His thoughts were clear as he and Luminous walked through the forest where his adventure began. He still wore the clothes given to him in Melodious. They were now dirty from the grime in Asebeia.

George was sad to leave and sorry not to say goodbye to Astrid, who, he thought, was the coolest girl he had ever met. *I suppose that's what dream girls are: all the best girls in school rolled into one; bright, brave, good-looking and definitely not soppy*!

'It is time for me to depart now, George. There is the road.' Luminous pointed to the tree George had rested against so long ago.

'I thought I'd wake up here.' His face was downcast.

'Cheer up, George.' Luminous returned to his fiery form. 'You can take comfort in knowing that you and your father will be friends again.' He spread his six wings and rose above the forest, the light of his glory filling the sky.

George clutched at his chest. A sudden sharp pain pierced it. He gasped for breath. The air slowly departed from his lungs, his legs gave way and he fell against the tree by the side of the road.

Chapter Sixteen

WAKING UP

George couldn't wake up properly. Strange visions filled his confused mind. He slipped in and out of consciousness. Every time he opened his eyes, he saw blurred images through a heavy mist. The golden glow of Luminous gave way to a mass of colours; yellow, green, white and blue. Blue lights flashed round and round, dancing to the wail of a siren. An oxygen mask was over his nose and mouth. Vaguely, he was aware of yellow shapes moving about him. Darkness descended once more.

The next time George opened his eyes, he saw a familiar face.

'Mum?' whispered George. She squeezed him tightly and he gained strength from her loving embrace. A tube pulled on his left arm.

'What's that for?'

'It's for the medicine in that bag.'

George looked up to where she was pointing and saw a transparent plastic bag hung above his head; clear liquid flowed down the tube and into his wrist.

'It's called a drip,' his mother said. 'I won't be long, George – I've got to fetch the nurse and phone your father to tell them that you're awake.'

His mother left and a young nurse with red hair came to

the foot of the bed. She beamed at George,

'Well, young man, you've had a long sleep.' She read some notes, and then took his temperature. Next, she put a different mask over his face and flicked a switch on the panel above his head. A pleasant tasting mist entered the mask.

'Breathe normally, George; this will make your chest feel less sore.' As he breathed in the mist, the pain fled away and his chest felt wonderful.

'It's called a nebuliser,' the nurse explained. 'It's all your inhalers rolled into one, only much more effective. When this little capsule is empty, press this button and I'll get you some toast.'

She pointed to the capsule and put a button, attached to a cable, into George's right hand. 'You do want some toast, don't you?' He shook his head. 'Toast will help your tummy feel better.' George shook his head again, he felt queasy.

'What about juice then?' In reply George nodded. 'So that's a yes! I'll bring some toast just in case you change your mind and a jug of juice – unless you would like a cup of tea?' George screwed up his face in disgust. 'Okay,' said the nurse. 'No tea! Don't speak, George, or the nebuliser won't be as effective.'

The nurse bounced down the corridor just as George's mother returned. She held his hand as she chatted about the family, giving him news of Jacqueline, John and May.

George frowned and asked,

'Why are you telling me about them as if I've been away a long time?'

'You mustn't talk yet, George,' reminded his mother. 'The truth is, you have been in hospital for ten days.' George's eyes widened in surprise. His mother continued,

'Yes, George, it is well over a week since you were found slumped against a tree, a little way from the roadside. You have been very ill. It's a good job your father called the police when you didn't come home. Anything could have happened to you out in that forest.'

'It did happen! I had the most amazing dream ever. It was so real and …'

'You can tell me later. What's that gurgling noise?'

'It's this nabuliser thingy,' said George.

'That's a nebuliser thingy,' said the nurse who had returned with a plate of hot buttered toast and a jug of cold juice. The delicious smell of the toast tempted George to remove the mask and to nibble on it but he didn't eat it all. The nurse asked to speak to his mother and though they talked quietly, George could hear what was said. Apparently, the police wanted to speak with him right away. His mother refused, saying that they could come in the morning, after her son had rested.

George's father came immediately he heard that George was awake. They gave each other a warm and friendly hug. George didn't need to hear his father saying sorry, nor did he have to say 'I forgive you.' The hug said it for them.

His mother told him, 'You were missing for seven hours. We were frantic with worry but a couple driving along the country road saw you lying against a tree; they called the police. You were very weak from your asthma and you've got a severe chest infection.'

'That's enough for now,' said his father, handing a parcel to him. 'This is to make your stay in hospital less boring.'

George unwrapped the present. It was a portable DVD player and some movies. George gratefully accepted the gift. He thanked his parents, knowing that they couldn't really afford the present. Just then the nurse came to give George another nebuliser and suggested that his parents should get some rest themselves. Instead, they sat beside the bed all night as they had done throughout the past ten days.

When George awoke the next day, he didn't know which was worse, being ill, or being poked about by doctors who talked over him as if he weren't there. The police came in the afternoon. They asked George many questions, not only about being thrown off the bus, but also about the school in general. They had a special interest in Mr Stenching. George's mother asked them to leave when she saw how tired and distressed he was getting.

Hospital routine was very dull. George was glad of the DVD player, although it was the friendship of the nurses and the care of his parents that really helped him to cope. His appetite slowly returned during the week, but he didn't like the hospital food. He was glad of the supply of chocolate digestive biscuits his parents had stashed in the locker beside the bed. George was taught how to cope with his asthma and how to use the new inhalers he had been given.

It was the day before he left the hospital when George's parents came to give him some good news. His father was very excited. He held up the local newspaper and showed George the headline: 'DEPUTY HEAD ARRESTED!'

'Listen to this, George,' he said eagerly, ''Parents, whose children attend Dunhill Senior School for boys, were in shock today when they learnt that the fifty-year-old school may be closed down.''

'Wow!' exclaimed George. 'That's brilliant!'

'There's a lot more,' replied his father, looking down the columns, 'blah, blah, blah. Ah, here it is! 'The decision to close the school permanently depends on the results of an enquiry to be held in the New Year. A surprise inspection revealed shocking standards in the way the school is run. The inspection followed a police investigation of allegations concerning the persistent bullying of children at the hands of certain teachers. The most disturbing aspect of the investigation was the arrest last night of the deputy head, Mr Stenching.''

'BRILLIANT!' interrupted George for the second time. His mouth was wide open as his father continued to read.

'Where was I? Oh yes, here it is. 'Mr Stenching faces charges of cruelty towards many boys during his ten years at the school. If convicted, he could be facing a long prison sentence. The head teacher, Mr Mole, who has been criticised for his short-sighted leadership, was not available for comment.

Another facing the possibility of prison is the driver of the school bus. Mr Liam Smith was arrested on charges of endangering the life of an eleven-year-old boy. He allegedly threw the boy off the bus, forcing him to walk a gruelling seven-mile journey in the pouring rain. The asthmatic boy (who cannot be named for legal reasons) nearly died of pneumonia.''

'They don't half exaggerate things,' George said, thoroughly enjoying himself. 'Er... what does 'allegedly' mean?'

'The paper is being careful by saying that he did throw you off the bus but they can't prove it yet.' explained his mother.

'Oh!'

'What is certain,' she added, 'is that justice will be done.'

The next day, George was overjoyed to leave the hospital. May was home for the holidays. One afternoon George persuaded her to play "hide and seek". They used to play this game a lot when they were much younger and it felt great to do something ordinary like this. May soon became bored though.

'I've had enough! I'm going to play Zillah on my Eibsae.'

'You're going to play what? On what?'

'Zillah – the game on my Eibsae!' Saying this, she pulled a tiny video game out of her pocket, putting phones into her ears while she turned it on.

'Oh that!' said George, 'Where did you get it from anyway?'

'Pardon?' she removed one of the ear phones.

'I asked where you got it from.'

'From a friend at school; it was a Christmas present; now get lost! I'm nearly on level ninety-five.'

George watched her go to her room, her eyes glazing over as she lost herself in the game. He sighed heavily,

'This is weird; she was just like this in my dream.' Just then his eye caught sight of something in the cupboard he'd been hiding in. It was a black bag containing some familiar clothing – a pair of tough boots, jeans, a sweatshirt and a black jacket. These were the clothes given to him in Melodious for his mission to Asebeia. George thought,

I must have seen these clothes before and dreamt about wearing them.

What he couldn't explain away were the cards he received on Christmas Eve. One was totally unexpected. It was from Helen Risdale. She wished George a happy Christmas and wrote at the foot of the card,

'Thanks for everything.' The surprise at getting a card from the former bully was nothing compared to the shock the letter from Glen gave him.

Dear George,

I had a weird dream the other week and you were in it. I was buried in a pit up to my neck. A horrible monster kept me a prisoner; it had many ugly heads but the worst was called Frame-up. I had been feeling guilty about my Mum and Dad splitting up. I thought it was all my fault.

Imagine my surprise when you turned up with a girl called Astrid. You got me out of the pit and helped me to realise that I am not to blame for my parents' divorce after all. The really strange thing is that when I woke up I didn't feel guilty anymore. And I don't blame myself for their bust up. The other thing is, I don't hate them now. I don't know what is going to happen in the future, but I know that things are going to get better.

Anyway George, I wanted to thank you even if it was a dream. I know that your friendship has helped me. My parents are sending me to that boarding school your sister goes to. I'll see you when you visit her – isn't that great? Have a brilliant Christmas. Your pal, Glen.

George showed the letter to his mother, who simply said,

'Fancy that!' He couldn't help noticing the twinkle in her eye. He spent the rest of that day trying to work out how three people could have the same dream. George's mind was distracted by the arrival of his brother, John. Jacqueline also came in the evening. Everyone was looking forward to the Christmas dinner George's father was preparing.

George's mother decided to tell her children that their father had been suffering from a terrible depressive illness due to his experience in the Middle East. John understood right away, having served in a submarine during the conflict. At his wife's insistence, their father showed them the medals he had been awarded for saving the lives of others. He went back into the kitchen when she began to relate the story George had heard from Daionas.

George didn't stay for the story, because he saw how awkward his father felt, so he went to help him make the Christmas pudding. George was busy licking out the bowl, when his father told him that they would be moving after Christmas.

'This posting was always to be a temporary one. There's a special hospital here on the base and I was sent there to be helped. The RAF was giving me time to recover and see if I was fit to return to work or not. Well, I am fit to return to work now and I've decided to accept the new posting. My commanding officer was very kind to me; he said that the RAF didn't want to lose me. I suppose it has something to do with the medals.'

'I bet it's more than the medals, Dad.'

'Well, anyway, we'll be moving to an RAF base in Scotland – don't know which one yet – but we're going home, George!'

George was thrilled at the news, because it meant that whatever happened, he would never return to Dunhill School. A loud crash followed by a scream came from the living room. One of the swords his father collected had fallen off the wall.

'I wish you would destroy these horrible things!' shouted George's mother when they entered the room.

'I promise to sell them, don't worry,' answered George's father, a little embarrassed. He added, 'I didn't realise what the depression was making me do; I had the feeling that I needed the swords for protection.'

'Protection from what?' asked John. His father shrugged his shoulders in reply.

Because of the lack of rooms in that tiny house, sleeping arrangements were very complicated. George shared his room with John, who slept on the top bunk bed. May and Jacqueline were in their parents' room while mother and father slept downstairs on the sofa that converted into a double bed.

George tossed and turned in his sleep. He dreamt that there was an evil presence in the house – the nightmares had returned...

Chapter Seventeen

THE SWORD OF DAIONAS

I'm back in the nightmare, thought George. *Something's in the house*. In a daze, he put on his dressing gown and slippers. He walked silently down the stairs, opened the door to the living room and allowed his eyes to adjust to the dim light coming through the curtains from the street outside.

The sight that greeted him was very odd. His mother was hiding under the dining table, opposite the kitchen. George approached the sofa bed. His father was soaked in sweat and moaning in his sleep. He didn't respond when George shook him. *I remember this dream – it's the one where Zenobiel tries to kidnap Dad. That must have been a warning from Daionas – what did He say? 'I will give you the power to defeat Zenobiel.' I have to trust the King of Light*.

Two giant claws dug into the back of the sofa. The vile head of Zenobiel appeared above the sleeping man.

A serpent's tongue flashed out of the cruel mouth, licking the face of George's father.

'Leave him alone!' yelled George. 'My Dad's a citizen of Melodious and you have no right to him now. I, on the other hand, have been given the right to stop you.' The hideous creature hissed at George.

'You feeble child! How dare you order me! I am the King of shadowsss and I have come to claim my own.'

'No,' replied George, whose intense anger overcame his terror. 'You are the king of lies and you have no claim over him. I tell you the truth; Daionas has given me the power to stop you. Flee now, or taste the edge of His sword!'

There was fear in Zenobiel's eyes. He snarled at George,

'I sssee no sword of Daionas in your hand.'

George sang the song in reply. Without warning, his voice left him. With his right claw, Zenobiel made the motion of pulling something out of George's mouth. At the same time, the other claw pushed the bed aside. It turned over completely. George's father woke up. He was appalled when he saw Zenobiel.

'William!' called his wife, 'Come here, quick!' He darted across the room on his hands and knees, joining his wife under the table.

Zenobiel had changed since George saw him last. He was much smaller now, but having a two metre monstrosity in your living room is still terrifying. The scorpion body was loose and rattled about as the beast moved its legs. The tail was more snakelike. The head was dented just above the eyes. The bloodshot eyes paralysed George with an evil stare. The talons of the claw grasped the air as if pulling George's vocal chords from his throat.

He was desperately trying to sing the Song of the Seraphim, but no sound came out of his mouth. The sword of Daionas did not appear in his hand, but he held his ground, reaching for one of his father's swords off the wall. Zenobiel matched his movements like a shadow, taking another sword at the same time as George. Both were poised for a duel.

George aimed a blow at the claw that was taking his voice away. Zenobiel's sword blocked it. The creature made a savage thrust for George's heart. He dived out of the way.

The Christmas tree was wrecked as the monster fell into it. In his mind, George called for Daionas while he ducked and dived away from his opponent's blade.

Zenobiel hit everything in the room except George. Chairs were hacked to pieces, ornaments smashed into little bits, pictures torn from the walls. For one wonderful moment, George managed to disarm the creature. The massive sharp claws lunged at George's head, but they dug into the wall behind him, gouging out great lumps of plaster. Zenobiel reached easily for another sword.

George's mother finally saw why her son wasn't singing the song, so, from under the now battered table, she started to sing. Her angelic voice filled the room, making Zenobiel freeze in dread. Immediately, George's voice returned. The evil beast howled in a vain attempt to drown out the song.

The mighty sword of Daionas appeared in a brilliant shaft of light. George took what was his to wield by right. Zenobiel made a thrust to cut off George's head – it was too late, sparks flew as his enemy's sword smashed his to bits, scattering it over the carpet.

Zenobiel went wild with rage. One by one, he grabbed weapons off the wall. Swords, knives and daggers were tossed at George, but he held himself like an expert cricketer, using the sword of fire to deflect all the weapons hurled at him. His careful aim protected his parents; weapons whizzed over them harmlessly.

Zenobiel lashed out with a curved dagger, slashing George's arm. He dropped the sword, clutched the wound, trying to stop the bleeding. Dizzy with pain, he fell against the china cabinet. Zenobiel tossed the dagger at George – it whizzed past his ears, smashing into the cabinet. George got to his feet, took off his dressing gown and ripped off his pyjama sleeve, wrapping it around the wounded arm.

Zenobiel stooped to snatch the sword of Daionas. George hurled the dagger at him; it flew over its head, crashing through the television screen. A piercing scream shook the walls.

Zenobiel was clutching a smoking claw. When he had touched the handle of the sword it had burnt him. George understood.

'You can't use your enemy's sword. You are not Daionas's equal, Zenobiel.'

This fact overcame all fear. George fought against the pain in his arm and glowed with strength. He deliberately took slow steps towards Zenobiel, who was seized with terror. He picked up the sword and spoke with authority.

'Daionas is your master, your king and your utter doom!'

Zenobiel cowered in the corner of the room. George advanced towards him. 'I have already told you that Daionas commanded me to use His sword and prevent you from taking my father. I will give you a choice, though you don't deserve it. Either leave now, or feel the sting of this mighty weapon!'

Zenobiel's answer was to dart at George, who brought the sword down upon the creature's back. The armoured crust broke in two. Zenobiel wriggled free, revealing the glistening body of a serpent. It made a feeble attempt at mocking George, by saying,

'I was discarding that shell anyway. You have done me a service, George.'

'I'll do you another one,' he said. 'I'll put you out of your misery!'

With lightning speed and tremendous force, George plunged the sword straight into the wound on Zenobiel's skull. He let go of the sword, which embedded itself deep in Zenobiel's head. The foul fiend twisted in agony. Smoke filled the room. The creature's body hissed into flame. For a second or two, only the high-pitched scream remained as Zenobiel melted into shadow. All was quiet at last.

The shimmering sword hovered in the air with its blade downwards. It faded but the clear voice of Daionas was heard, saying,

'Well done, George. Well done.'

George stood for a while, looking at the scene of destruction. His father's collection of swords and knives were scattered in pieces across the room.

'Well,' he gasped, 'Mum... got... her wish after all!' The quiet in the room made George aware of the agony in his arm and the blood soaking his pyjamas. He thought, *I wonder why I haven't woken up*?

The light came on and George's mother approached him with a bowl of clean water and bandages. George jumped in surprise. His mother perceived his thoughts.

'I suppose you still insist that this has all been a dream.'

George slumped into a wrecked chair. His father held up his hand to show a gold ring on his finger. His mother did the same, and for the first time, George noticed the ring of Melodious next to her wedding ring. She had a crystal jar of ointment – the same ointment Astrid had used on him when in Asebeia. The soothing cream began to heal the wound the moment it was rubbed in.

'But... that's from Melodious,' he gasped.

'So is this,' replied his father, taking a ring out of his pocket and handing it to George.

'Read the inscription on the inside.' George did so. It said, *George William Tweedie, citizen of Melodious, now and forever more*. George's mother explained,

'We took it off you when you were in hospital to prevent it from being stolen and to stop you from learning the truth before you were ready to hear it.'

'So...' mumbled George, 'everything has been real?'

'Yes,' they replied.

'I wasn't dreaming?'

'No, you weren't.'

'Oh!'

The last hours of that night were spent in answering many questions. George's mother answered those she could.

'After all,' she said, 'I don't know everything. I can tell you that Daionas has been sending people into Asebeia since time began. His chosen method is to send one person for another. Your Grandmother was sent for me. I was sent for Mr Johnson. Astrid was sent for you, and...' She paused for dramatic effect; 'you surprised us all.'

'Why?'

'Because Daionas decided to send you not for one person...'

'But for three!' put in George. 'A friend, an enemy and my own Dad.'

'Thank you son, you made me well again.'

'I didn't, the King of Light did.'

'But He did it with your help.'

'When can I return to Melodious?'

'Whenever you wish,' said his mother, 'Daionas told you that.'

'When I was in Melodious, my asthma had gone. Why did it return?' It was George's father who answered, placing his hand gently on his son's shoulder.

'Did Daionas promise that you would be healed?'

'No.'

'Then you have no right to be disappointed.'

'Your dad is correct, George,' added his mother. 'But you can be certain that every promise Daionas does make, He will keep. He did give you the power to fight Zenobiel and I'm hoping that Daionas will send you back to Asebeia to rescue more prisoners from that evil city, especially May.'

George gave her a puzzled look.

'Didn't you realise,' she explained, 'that May's still there? That video game she's got – it's called an Eibsae – what's that an anagram of?'

'I don't know I've never been good at anagrams.'

'Asebeia – it's an anagram of Asebeia – like I said, she's still there.'

'But,' said George, 'she's in her room; how can she be in two places at once?' George's father answered him.

'Asebeia is in an invisible, spiritual world, George. Her body may be here but her spirit is trapped in darkness.

Remember, what's on the inside of a person is made visible in Rûah. Don't try to work it out; just be ready.'

George quietly thought about it all before saying,

'I remember when I first met Zenobiel, the day we moved from Fordale. He told me that my dad was his and my sister was his, but I didn't understand at the time. When will I rescue her then?'

'Daionas will send for you when He's ready,' said his mother, 'but now we must tidy up.'

George looked at the devastation.

'What a mess! How are we going to explain this to the others?'

In answer there was a knock at the door. George's father opened it. Luminous and other Seraphim in human form entered the room. They cleared up all the mess, repaired the damaged walls and replaced everything with new and better furniture. There was a new Hi-Fi system along with a collection of CDs.

When the transformation of the room was finished, Luminous beamed at them.

'A present from the King. Happy Christmas!' He and the other Seraphim sang their song to them. The room was bathed in a warm golden glow. The Seraphim spread their wings and departed. Their voices hung on the air. After the Seraphim left, George whispered in awe,

'I thought I couldn't be surprised anymore.'

Chapter Eighteen

NEW HOME, NEW SCHOOL – NEW ADVENTURES?

Dear Glen,

Thanks for your letter. I hope you had a good Christmas. Ours was the best ever. We were really close as a family this year and never bothered with the TV. We moved to Scotland on January 17th.

Where we live is a cold place, but the people are warm and friendly. I know it's very unusual to have two moves close together, but it had something to do with Dad's illness. He's much better now. It's like old times in our new house, which is bigger than the last one. Dad's like a big kid really. He and Mum got me a train set for Christmas and Dad's been playing with the trains more than me!

John's gone back to sea now, Jacqueline is hoping to visit in March, and May is going back to school. It's great news about you coming back to England and attending the same school as May. Mum says that you can stay with us on leave weekends.

When you do, I'll tell you all about your dream. I'm starting school tomorrow. It looks quite good. I'll let you know how I get on.

See you soon, Your Pal, George.

George woke up on Tuesday morning feeling nervous, but excited about making new friends. His new school was better than any he had been to before. He met the head teacher who welcomed him and took him to his class to meet his new form teacher. The classroom was empty, because the school day had not begun.

'This is George Tweedie. I've seen his work. He's a gifted artist and a good writer.' She smiled as she added, 'Needs help with maths and computer skills though. George, I hope you will feel at home here.'

She left the room and George chatted with the teacher before being shown to his desk, just as the other children came into the classroom. He was busy putting his books away and didn't notice the pupil approaching the desk. A book thudded in front of him. George was startled. He looked up at the girl who had sat down next to him. He was amazed when he saw her dark skin, ponytail and mischievous grin. Her big brown eyes sparkled with fun.

'Hello, George, Daionas sent me – we've got to go back and rescue May,' said Astrid, giggling at the astonished look on her friend's face.

Author's Note

This book was first published in 2009 under the title of *The Song of the Seraphim*. I was never really happy with it and felt it had some failings. I listened to those readers who were good enough to point out the story's strengths and weaknesses and worked on a revision.

The most noticeable change is in the title. I thought *George and the Monster Inside* gave a more accurate description of the story than the original title but others disagreed, so I compromised and used *The Song of the Seraphim* as a series title for the books to follow. This is my first novel, so I know it isn't perfect but hope you enjoyed it anyway.

I have often been asked if this is a Christian book. The answer is yes and no. Yes, it reflects my Christian beliefs and the great story of the Bible. No, in that it is not explicitly Christian. What I wanted to do was write an exciting adventure story that would be enjoyed by anyone, regardless of their beliefs or lack of them.

More details of this book's journey can be found on my website and Facebook page:

www.andrewghill.com

www.facebook.com/the.books.ofA.G.Hill

About the Author

Like George, A G Hill was born on an RAF base and moved a lot during his childhood, attending many different schools. He was also bullied at school with children teasing him about the gaps in his teeth and calling him, "tombstone".

However, in one school this rather cruel nickname became a badge of honour when friends called him "tombstone" for entertaining them with scary stories.

When leaving school, A.G. vowed never to have anything to do with schools but he ended up as a schools worker with the London City Mission for 19 years!

His love of storytelling was rekindled and in addition to telling Bible stories, he created many of his own. When a prolonged period of ill health forced him out of work, he turned a disappointment into an opportunity by writing this, his first novel.

He now lives in Aberdeen, Scotland with his wife and an ever growing collection of classical music, film soundtracks and books.

Acknowledgements

Thank you to all who have read the first edition of this book and given their honest opinions, they have helped me to fine-tune the present work.

Thanks go to Patricia Schiavone, the editor of the first edition, and to Tony Maude, the editor of this second edition.

A special thank you to Rob Rowe, the station manager at G4G radio, who kept urging me to read it on his station and publish another edition.

Made in the USA
Charleston, SC
20 November 2014